Lynching
(A Collection of Short Stories)

Alok Kumar Satpute

Ukiyoto Publishing

All global publishing rights are held by

Ukiyoto Publishing

Published in 2024

Content Copyright © Alok Kumar Satpute

ISBN 9789362694447

All rights reserved.
No part of this publication may be reproduced, transmitted, or stored in a retrieval system, in any form by any means, electronic, mechanical, photocopying, recording or otherwise, without the prior permission of the publisher.

The moral rights of the author have been asserted.

This work blends fact and fiction. While some elements may be inspired by real-life events, names, characters, businesses, places, locales, and incidents have been created by the author's imagination or utilised fictitiously. Any resemblance to actual persons, living or dead, or actual events may exist but is not indicative of a direct correlation.

.

This book is sold subject to the condition that it shall not by way of trade or otherwise, be lent, resold, hired out or otherwise circulated, without the publisher's prior consent, in any form of binding or cover other than that in which it is published.

www.ukiyoto.com

My wife and son

Contents

Mob Lynching	1
Racism	3
Civil War	4
Justice	6
Slave	7
Danger	9
Atheist	10
Country	12
Poison	13
Intruders	15
Impotent	16
Opium	18
Slave	19
Existence	20
Lust	21
Festive	22
Male	23
Sacrifice	24
Justice	25
Cultured	26
Progressive	27
Religious women-1	28
Religious women -2	29
The most dangerous animal	30
Politics	31
Strong	32
Pandemic	33
Majority	34

Ascetic	35
Caste and Status	36
A Shrewd Ruler	36
Predictions	37
Mahatma Gandhi' Goat	37
Jihad	38
Solution	39
Conversion	39
Dalits	40
Tit for tat	40
Opium	41
Convenient	41
An Empty Mind	42
Message	42
Genies	43
Communal	43
Nationalist	44
National Servant	45
Slavery	46
Man	47
System	48
Ramrajya	49
Convenient-2	49
Brahmin	50
Ash	50
Sevakpur	51
Bankrupt	52
A Leader Country	53
Bankrupt	53
Sin	54
Jhatka	54

Lust	55
Future	55
Turnes	56
God and Satan	56
Reaction	57
Ray of Hope	57
Backlash	58
Conflict	59
Two incidents	59
Truth	60
Treatment	60
Leaders	61
Son	62
Dogs	63
A modern man	63
Life	64
Blind	64
Status	65
Mother	65
Practical	66
Patriotism	66
Intentions	67
Tommy	68
Salute	69
Think Positive	70
Moksha (Salvation)	71
Destiny	72
Lynching	73
Nationalist	73

Identification	74
Ghanta(Bell)	76
Marital	77
Evaluation	78
Assessment	78
Market	79
Theif	80
Relations	81
Relations	82
Radiation	83
Insecurity	83
Irresponsible	84
Jamaati	85
Brothel	86
Judgment	87
Opportunists	87
Logic	88
Break-up	89
Guarantee	91
superstition	92
Comparison	93
Marital	94
Conclusion	95
Thugs	96
Truth	96
Calculation	98
Needs	99
Prostitutes	99
Belief	100
Law	100

Bankrupted	101
Net	101
Custom	102
Pati Parmeshvar	102
Hypocrite	103
Correlation	104
Hypocrite	104
Flight	105
Defeat	105
Bazaar (Market)	106
Credit	106
Bankrupted	107
Brahmhatya	108
Illegal Faith	109
Conviction	110
Democracy	110
Status	111
Conspiracy	111
Views	112
Gods of riots	112
Gandhi-Jayanti	113
Pander	114
Donations	115
Status	116
Revolution	116
Laughter	117
Democracy	117
Pind-daan	118
Fusion	119
Wisdom	119

Corrigendum	120
Ash	120
Improbity	121
Improbity	121
Slavery	122
Public interest	122
System	123
Captured	123
Status	124
Insecurity	125
Eunuch	125
Lesson	126
Bitter truth	126
Speed	126
Character	127
Honour of needs	128
Mother	128
World Renewal	129
Knowledge Selling	129
Defect	130
Talent Hunt	131
Impotent	132
Taliban	133
Dalit	133
Blackmail	134
Compromise	134
The biggest religious person	135
Eunuchs	135
Pride	136
Adopted Daughter	137

Worship	137
Competition	138
Double Status	138
Achievements	139
Bazaar(Market)	139
Postmortem	140
True Lover	140
Auction	141
Business	141
Offering	142
Frustration	143
Nervous Breakdown	144
Curse	144
Manhood	145
Democracy	146
Elites	146
Address	147
Dignity	147
Shop Keeping	148
Caste feeling	149
Business	150
About the Author	*152*

Mob Lynching

Arif Mohammad was walking quickly on the sidewalk. Just the day before, a mob lynching had occurred in his city.

A group of university students was marching on the road to protest the lynching.

Arif shuddered remembering the lynching that had taken place the previous day. He recalled how a mob had beaten up a Muslim man on suspicion of theft. The crowd that was beating him demanded that he chant *"Jai Shri Ram"* repeatedly. Being afraid, Arif did not stay in that area for long. He later learned that the mob had killed the man. The memory of the scene made him break out in cold sweat.

Suddenly, Arif noticed a blind man who seemed to be attempting to cross the road. Arif approached him and asked, "Surdasji, do you need help crossing the road?"

"Yes", the blind man replied.

Arif took his hand and guided him across the road. By this time, the protest had moved ahead.

"What's all the noise about?" the blind man asked.

"Yesterday, a mob lynching occurred in the city. The procession is a protest by college students," Arif explained.

"What is mob lynching?" the blind man inquired.

"It's when a person is attacked and killed by a mob," Arif answered.

"That's very wrong and cowardly. Who was killed?" the blind man asked.

"Tanveer Ahmed", Arif replied.

"Then the mob is absolutely right. These Muslims are very conservative. They should be sent to Pakistan", the blind man stated.

Hearing this, Arif trembled. The blind man's hand began to feel like it was pricking him sharply as if he were holding a knife by the blade instead of the handle. He felt as though his hand was bleeding.

When they reached the other side, Arif noticed an open gutter. For a moment, he considered throwing the "knife" into the gutter, but then his inner voice told him, "Don't be a coward."

He decided to listen to his inner voice and quickly parted ways with the blind man, moving forward at a rapid pace.

*Surdas - Polite terms for individuals with visual impairments

Jai Shri Ram - This Hindu religious slogan is currently being used to intimidate minorities

Racism

(At a pet store that sells supplies for dogs)

Customer: Can I have a leash for a three-month-old puppy, please?

Shopkeeper: Just the leash or do you need a chain as well?

Customer: I need both, please.

Shopkeeper: Is your puppy a Labrador, Bulldog, or Pomeranian?

Customer: I'm sorry, what does the breed of the dog have to do with the leash?

Shopkeeper: Sir, I have designer leashes and chains that are tailored to specific breeds of dogs. They are priced above five hundred rupees.

Customer: Well, my puppy is a local breed.

Shopkeeper: In that case, you can buy this simple leash for only fifty rupees. You can also use a nylon rope to walk your puppy. The shopkeeper said with disdain.

Civil War

In that jungle, the king lion was killed by a hunter. His cub was not capable to rule, so the jackals took over the power of that jungle. Wolves and hyenas were also members of their cabinet. Because of the heron's meditative posture, the fox's cunningness, and the crocodile's tears, which left a strong impression, they were appointed as advisors.

While ruling the jackals also realized that they would not be able to rule for a long time, so one day the king jackal called a meeting of the cabinet and advisors.

During the meeting, the king stated, "Friends, history shows that under the dynasty rule, capable jackals like us did not have many opportunities to rule the jungle. Now that we have been given a chance by luck, we must strive to rule the jungle for at least the next fifty years. We need to create conditions such that if we cannot rule the forest, then no one else can. Now, I want to hear your ideas on how we can make this possible.

"If we only kill the lion cub, we will have no rival", suggested Minister Wolf.

"No, this could lead to rebellion against us", the king said.

"Then we should start calling the lion cub a kitten so that he starts thinking of himself as a kitten", suggested the cunning advisor fox.

"We will recruit the lion's loyalists into our party, and anyone who does not agree to join will be declared a jungle traitor. Additionally, we will create division among all wild animals by labeling their characteristics as their shortcomings", suggested Heron.

The king jackal heeded all the advice. Hatred began to spread in the jungle. All animals were labeled with different analogies, such as snakes being likened to creeping creatures, leopards being called cowards that hunt secretly, Burmese pythons being referred to as foreigners, deer being seen as fools, and porcupines being described as thorny animals.

They began to taunt each other, leading to fights among themselves. Even the fishes in rivers and ponds started fighting and dying based on color and shape. The herons no longer needed to concentrate because dead fish were easily available to them. The crocodile also feasted and then started shedding tears over the deteriorating condition of the forest. The lion cub continued to see itself as a kitten.

The hyena had amassed a collection of bones and would eat them while laughing dangerously.

Civil war had broken out in the jungle.

Justice

(In a closed room)

Investigating Officer: On which basis did you encounter those eight accused?

Police: Sir, they were hazardous criminals for society, so due to public sentiments, we encountered all eight of them... We are not at all sorry about this, but are happy.

Investigating Officer: What "public" and What "sentiments"? Are you talking about the "public" who videoed the crime instead of trying to stop it? Or are you talking about that public, who justifies the crime committed by his "community" and celebrates it? This is not "public" but a "crowd".

Police: Due to so much delay in getting justice people have lost faith in the judicial system, what could we do in such a situation, sir. how to get justice after all?

Investigating Officer: Do encounter, but instead of stopping the crime, on the impotent people who made videos of it and the crowd who encouraged and celebrated the crime. Only then will there be justice.

Slave

I was familiar with a person from the Dalit caste who lived in my neighborhood. He concealed his caste, as Dalits often do. This is a common practice of Dalits. He identified himself as Kshatriya (upper caste), and since he was from a distant village people accepted him as a Kshatriya. He always displayed a saffron religious flag on his house for recognition. He would walk several kilometers carrying Kanwar and chanting Bol Bam slogans. He frequently organized katha in his house. He would wash the feet of Brahmin Maharajs and show disdain for Dalits.

Every holiday, he and his family would visit nearby religious places. He already visited all the important religious places, such as Jagannath Puri, Vaishnav Devi, and Jwalamukhi Devi. He had also travelled to Kailash Mansarovar and was involved in the Ayodhya temple movement. He even brought a brick from there, which he kept in his worship room. He would recount his religious journeys to the neighbourhood as if he had returned from a victorious battle. I, too, considered him a Kshatriya (upper caste) for many years until a friend from the same village revealed his actual caste. This revelation made me indignant.

This summer, he planned to visit the Somnath temple, and his children enthusiastically shared the news.

One day, as I was reading the newspaper, I came across a news about a Dalit man who had been attacked by a group of people at the Somnath temple, accused of stealing Prasad. It saddened me to see that Dalits are still being discriminated against in this day and age.

A few months later, the Dalit man's family returned but he was not with them. His wife came to our house one day, crying uncontrollably.

When we inquired, she told us that her husband had been killed outside the temple. There was a sign outside the temple forbidding the entry of Shudras/Dalits, but her husband identified himself as a Kshatriya.

A Pandit from their village recognized him and riled up a crowd, accusing him of desecrating the temple, which led to his lynching by the mob. Reports claimed that he was stealing Prasad.

*Shudras/Dalit - Untouchables , backward caste

Danger

"The people of religion A of the world should unite... religion A is in danger. Said the preacher of A religion."

'The people of religion B of the world should unite...B religion is in danger. The preacher of B religion scared them.

People of the C and D religions also cried out of danger.

Such and such nation is in danger. A big leader said while appealing for nationalism.

A casteist politician said that such and such caste is in danger.

Such and such language is in danger. The one doing language politics scared people in the name of the language.

Similarly, the people of such and such, so-and-so nation, caste, and language also played their tricks.

After a few days, a world war broke out in the world in the name of religion, nation, caste, and language. In the end, the existence of man came to an end. Only religion, nation, caste, and language remained, without human beings who had no worth.

Atheist

He was an orphan, having lost his parents when he was a child. Life had been a constant struggle for him as a result he had lost faith in God.

He was married to an orphan girl who was a believer. She believed that their past karma had led them to be orphans. She encouraged him to believe in some form of supreme power.

One day, at her insistence, he visited the largest temple in the city. However, as he approached the entrance, he noticed a sign stating that Shudras were not allowed. This led him to contemplate the four varnas of the Hindu religion, realizing that he did not belong to any of them. His caste was viewed differently in different parts of India, leaving him feeling confused and disheartened. He began to return when he noticed a Sufi tomb. There was a belief among the people that their wishes would be granted at that tomb. He stopped at the tomb and knelt in the courtyard. After some time, he bowed down repeatedly. Then a man approached and told him that he couldn't perform namaz there and should go to the mosque if he wanted to perform.

"What do people do there, then Bhai Jaan?" he asked.

"The shops nearby sell sheets of flowers(chadar) and other items. You can buy them and offer them here to make a wish", the man replied.

Why do people believe that their wishes will be granted when this tomb itself expects something from people" he murmured before leaving.

He had heard about Christianity and was drawn to the compassionate face of Jesus Christ and the statues of Mother Mary with a child. He turned towards the church and heard a priest saying something loudly. After some time, prayer started with dissonant voices and musical instruments. He got bored and left out.

He asked a man outside why there was so much noise in this church. The man looked at him and said, "You seem like a new convert. This is a Protestant church, and this is how prayer happens here. For a peaceful prayer, you should go to RC Church."

"What's the difference between the two?" he asked.

"They believe that Jesus wouldn't have been born without his mother, and we believe that Jesus had to be born, with or without his mother", the man explained.

"Okay, what is this tithe?" he asked before leaving.

"Tithing is donating at least ten percent of your income to the church each month," the man replied.

Saying, "exactly as extortion is done" he started to head home.

These experiences had transformed him from a potential atheist to a staunch atheist.

Country

Fewer people and more brokers were living in that vacant government housing colony. These brokers would give toffees to the children of nearby slums to break the windows of vacant houses. Apart from this, those brokers themselves would go at night and uproot doors, windows, grills, taps, and pipes. They would also climb onto the roof and pick up water tanks. These brokers had also opened hardware shops to sell these items.

Some brokers gained control of the keys of many owners' houses by promising to find them tenants, and they secretly turned those houses into brothels.

These brokers approach every new resident to ask about their issues. People believed that no one was as helpful as these brokers, and they became their loyal followers.

Over time, the colony became fully settled. The brokers became the wealthiest in the colony. It was clear that in the colony elections, these brokers held all the positions from President to Secretary. The residents of the colony were so impressed by their dedication to service that they were elected unopposed every time.

Today, the state of the nation has deteriorated ineptly like the housing colony.

Poison

"These Muslims should be deported to Pakistan."

'Why? What have they done?'

"All of them are terrorists."

'Oh! Now think about your Muslim friends from childhood till now and see what harm they have caused you.'

(Remembering those days)

" No, they did not harm me, even though we have close family relations with many Muslims. Many times they have even helped us, still..."

'Still what?'

"Those people are very fanatic. They do not eat the prasad given by us. From writing to washing their hands, everything they do is opposite to ours. Think about us, how generous we are, who go to the Mazars and offer chadars(sheets of flowers). We also participate in Muharram processions and pass under the Tajiya."

'What is the harm to you by their not eating prasad, way of writing and washing their hands oppositely?'

"Nothing!"

'Now listen to me. You do not offer a sheet at the Mazars because you are generous. You do not have faith in your Gods, so you go to the shrine in the hope of getting your wish fulfilled, and come out from under the Tajiya of Muharram in the hope of something auspicious happening. Well, leave it, just tell me whether you can employ a Muslim to cook food at your house. Come on, this is a big deal. Can you rent the vacant upper floor of your house to a Muslim? No...now think, every Muslim arranges separate vegetarian food for his vegetarian Hindu friends at every event. Now you tell me, do you arrange separate non-vegetarian food for your Muslim friends? Now you tell me, are you more fanatic or they?'

"What you are saying is hundred percent right, friend, but still..."

Muslims in India are a minority group that is often viewed with suspicion by the majority Hindu population

Intruders

Once upon a time, religion's influence became so significant that the world became divided based on religion. Countries began telling their minorities to return to their countries of origin.

Upon exploring world history, it was discovered that there is a very unequal division in the world. Minorities in some countries are majorities in others. Israel sided with the Jews, while the Middle East sided with the Muslims. European countries sided with Christians. History was distorted to suit their convenience. In America, immigrants with green cards were declared infiltrators and were asked to bring certificates from Columbus's descendants. In Aryavarta(India), distrust based on religion began to grow. Extreme distrust based on religion was growing in all countries. All countries began checking the capacity of their arsenals. The sounds of a Third World War on religious grounds began to be heard.

While the world was plotting destruction, atheist scientists were conducting experiments to save the world. An atheist scientist presented a time machine to the world. This time machine could take people to an era thousands of years ago. Even the religions that accused atheists of blasphemy were impressed by his intelligence, and the time machine was unanimously approved.

When America was visited thousands of years ago, it was found to be a country of Red Indians. African countries like Ethiopia, Sudan, and Burundi were inhabited only by tribals, and due to infiltrators, conditions of starvation had arisen there. All the countries were visited one by one. It was revealed that Mumbai-Dubai was an island of fishermen and Aryavarta(India) was also a country entirely of natives. Now all countries and religions have been proven to be infiltrators. Now they all seemed to be hiding their faces. It was understood that only the tribals who live in their fun completely devoid of religion are truly civilized and superior.

Impotent

It was a Sunday. Being over fifty, he was very upset by the protests happening in different parts of the country and he also wanted to take part in the protests.

Seeing the students being beaten, he felt that his life had been wasted because he couldn't do anything in his youth. Then he recollected an idiom–' morning comes when you wake up'. His blood started boiling.

He had no hope from his dead city. He checked the weather outside. Cold winds were blowing. He stayed lying down covered with a blanket. Suddenly he heard slogans of Zindabad-Murdabad outside.

He felt that perhaps his dead city had come to life and people had come out to protest. He came out full of excitement, he saw that a very long procession was passing in front of his house.

When he looked carefully, he found that in their hands were a photo of a Baba who was in jail for the crime of rape, and they were saying Zindabad (long live) to him and also saying Murdabad to the administration. He returned disappointed and then covered himself with a blanket and lied down.

After some time he suddenly realized that patriotic songs were being played somewhere in the distance. He felt that the sound was getting closer. Now Vande Mataram started playing. He started feeling that whether it happens or not, people have come out to protest.

When he came out, he saw that a lot of religious flags were kept in a cart, a loudspeaker fitted in the cart was playing, and the people walking behind that cart were distributing religious flags.

Thinking that he would not come out now, he went inside his blanket again. It had now been an hour since he was lying down. He was feeling sleepy. Suddenly he heard some sounds of Dhol-Manjire and Qawwali, as well as the sound of knocking on the door.

His heart started racing. Now surely someone or the other must have come asking to join the protest. He immediately reached outside and found many bearded men of Mustande(burly) type on the roadside holdng sheets and begging for offerings in some Mazar while from the other side, some people were coming closer playing drums and singing carols.

Vexedly he closed the door. Now he had completely understood that anything could happen in his dead city, except protests.

Opium

The king and his home minister understood the importance of opium. They imported high-quality opium using gold coins from the treasury, as the conditions in their country were not suitable for opium cultivation. They relied on their neighboring country, where opium was cultivated in abundance.

The public in the country was oppressed, and there were frequent rebellions against the monarchy. To maintain control, opium was imported from the neighboring country to intoxicate the people and prevent revolution.

The neighboring country began to realize the situation and raised the prices of opium. Concerned about the burden on the treasury, the king consulted his advisor, and a solution was found.

Following the advisor's suggestion, all print and electronic media were instructed to run programs on opium twenty-four hours a day. News, documentaries, debates, and other programs were to focus solely on opium. Any program on a different subject was considered treason.

Over time, the people of that country went into hallucination and the monarchy gained permanent recognition.

Slave

One day, Ramesh came across a medium-sized stray dog, slightly larger than a puppy, in a pitiful condition on the road. Feeling sorry for the dog, he picked it up and brought it home.

Upon seeing the stray dog, his wife became angry and asked why he brought up a stray dog. She expressed her desire to have a foreign-breed dog instead, which would give them a sense of pride and status in the colony.

Ramesh explained that the dog would serve as a guard and that we should not be concerned about its breed. His wife agreed but insisted that the dog should stay within its limits and not be given any special treatment.

Over time, Ramesh noticed that the dog was different from other dogs. It wagged its tail at a faster speed and would often visit the neighbors to make them feel as if it was hungry. The neighbors would offer food to the dog.

Ramesh also observed that the dog did not bark and would often sit at the neighbors' doors. He wondered about seeing this.

After two years, Ramesh's wife also grew fond of the dog. However, they felt embarrassed by its lack of barking and its behavior of accepting food from others.

Ramesh decided to train the dog to carry "Namaste" and "See you again" boards to welcome and bid farewell to guests. The dog learned the commands and would escort guests to and from the house.

One day, Ramesh's neighbors informed him that every guest who visited their house kicked the non-barking dog. They suggested that the dog should at least know how to bark, even if it couldn't bite.

In an attempt to teach the dog to bark, Ramesh and his wife tried to train it every day with a stick. However, the dog remained unaffected and even started growling at them.

Existence

Although I have many friends, I would like to mention only three of them here: Sarju, Subhash, and Vinu.

When I look at the achievements of all four of us in the last twenty-five years, I find that Sarju has made a good amount of capital by giving loans to the poor at ten percent monthly interest. He has very big commercial complexes and a Land-Rover car worth about Rs 1 crore.

Subhash is a very big officer and has also acquired a lot of wealth. He has purchased movable and immovable properties in different cities in the name of his relatives and servants. He has a BMW car worth sixty-seven lakhs.

I only have a housing board lower-income house and a motorcycle as my property.

Vinod has studied only till 12th and is a teacher in a primary school. He still lives in a rented house and has a bicycle in his name as a vehicle which has not been sold yet. I have known him since he used to receive Rs 500 as an honorarium for teaching. He has a fondness for wine and women.

Whenever I want to feel wealthy, I visit his house. I feel very happy when he comes to me in a vulnerable state and shares his struggles.

When I feel like giving advice, I call him and advise him to stay away from women and alcohol. This brings me great satisfaction.

To save and maintain my existence, I need Vinod, not Subhash or Sarju.

Lust

There was a timid type stray dog that lived on the street in front of Chhagan's house. Its territory was limited to just four or five houses on the street. Other dogs were dominant at both ends of the street.

Chhagan often observed that in the evenings, dogs from other neighborhoods would attack that dog, causing it to run around howling.

One day, Chhagan saw the dog roaming with a large group of stray dogs, four kilometers away from its usual street. This surprised him greatly.

He stopped to watch and noticed that a mating was taking place among the dogs. All the dogs in the pack were fighting among themselves, but none of them were backing down.

Furthermore, that timid dog was also fiercely involved in the fight. The fire of lust had broken all boundaries. All the dogs had become aggressive.

Festive

While walking from home to his office, Chandu saw a dead body wrapped in white clothes lying outside a house. Many men were standing nearby with mournful faces. Sounds of women crying were also coming from inside. Praying in his mind for the peace of that deceased soul, he moved ahead.

Returning from the office in the evening, he found that there was a festive atmosphere in the same house. The eating and drinking phase was going on. Men and women were dancing to the tunes of the DJ.

His steps stopped in surprise. When he asked a paan stall vendor about this unexpected incident, he came to know that the people of this house were mourning the death of their family member, thinking that he was alive and safe in another city. Someone else's body was handedover to them by the police based on mistaken identity. These peoplewere celebrating the survival of that member of their family.

Hearing this, Chandu was shocked and started thinking that at least someone had died. If they can't pray for the peace of that soul, then at least don't celebrate.

Male

You must visit such and such ashram. By going there, all five vices – lust, anger, ego, attachment, and greed – are eliminated. A seventy-year-old man said to a twenty-three-year-old young man.

I can't say about other vices, but I know one thing very well: it is absolutely impossible to control the "lust" vice. The young man replied.

Hey, what are you talking about, just look at me. It has only been five to six months since I started going to that ashram, and I have gained control over all other vices, including lust. The old man told him.

At your age, lust dies itself then how can you control it? The young man asked teasingly.

Oh no, It's not like that. We are also men. Many times our mind gets disturbed after seeing an attractive woman. That old man's manly ego was deeply hurt.

So, there's no age limit for bastardity. The young man was also not going to stay behind.

Heh, heh, heh, what can I say now, you are quite sensible yourself. The old man said, shyly.

Sacrifice

A stray dog used to roam around Dinesh's house. He would give him stale food. Although other people on his street also gave some food to that dog, The dog would often sit in front of Dinesh's house. When it rained, it would stand at the gate of Dinesh's house and Dinesh took it inside his house to save it from getting wet.

Gradually, a kingdom of that dog was established in that street. The dog did not even allow other dogs and cattle to roam in that street. At night, the dog remained very alert and kept watch.

If Dinesh watched him carefully many times, he realized that when the dog's stomach was full, he sat near the food and started growling from a distance if it saw any other animal coming towards the food. The dog didn't let any other dog eat its food.

Once, Dinesh saw that the dog was sitting guarding the food. Another dog was moving towards the food from a distance. Expecting a fierce fight between them, Dinesh started watching curiously. But his surprise knew no bounds when he saw that instead of fighting, the dog was letting the other dog eat the food comfortably. On the contrary, was watching it eating with great love. The dog was moving around it with his ears raised, licking it, and also making cooing sounds with its mouth. In a way, the dog was flattering it.

Dinesh was very surprised. He went a little closer and saw that the other dog was not a dog but a bitch. Dinesh suddenly realized that the mating season of dogs had arrived.

Justice

As Arun walked past a known shop, he noticed a signboard indicating that the shop was going to be auctioned.

He stopped and asked the neighboring shopkeeper about the travel agent's office that used to be there.

The shopkeeper informed him that the agent had gone bankrupt. The agent had purchased the shop with a bank loan, and now when he became a defaulter then the bank had taken possession of it and was preparing to auction it.

Hearing about the agent, Arun felt like he had traveled back in time fifteen years. The agent was a rude man. When Arun needed to go to Delhi for his child's heart operation, the agent demanded five times the normal fare for a railway reservation. When Arun protested that one should not take advantage of his dire situation, the agent callously replied that taking advantage in a dire situation is his business.

Arun pondered on the fact that in today's age of technology, train tickets can be easily booked online, and businesses that take advantage of people's dire situation are on the decline.

Cultured

"Yaar, this morning when I was heading to Gol Bazaar, I noticed a goat tied near a butcher's shop. The goat was looking around with its neck raised. When I returned from the market, I saw that the poor goat's neck had been cut. It made me feel sad."

"Brother, there's nothing that can be done about it. It's the fate of the goat to be slaughtered. That's why they say, 'How long will the goat's mother rejoice.'"

"Yes, that's true, but as I have seen the goat alive before its slaughter, I felt sorry for it. After all, kindness and compassion are human values. It's simply unbearable for someone like me who has religious beliefs and worships."

"You are right yaar, but what can we do now? By the way, why were you going to Gol Bazaar so early in the morning?"

"I was going to buy mutton. We always buy mutton from the butcher at the corner in Gol Bazaar. He gives us the tender meat from the goat's hindquarters."

Progressive

(On phone call)

"Hello, are you Mr. Suresh, President of Progressive Blood Donor Group?"

'Yes, that's me.'

"Sir, five friends who were going for a picnic have suffered serious injuriez in a road accident. I have brought them to the hospital in my car. I have admitted them to Arogya Hospital. Two of them need blood. I saw your location nearby, so I called you."

'Ok, what are their names?'

"Sir, the name of one of them is Asim and the other one said his name is Suresh Joshi."

'What is Asim's full name?'

"Sir, his full name is Asim Khan."

'Then forgive us, brother. We consider Muslims as Jihadis and we do not help them in any way. As far as Suresh Joshi is concerned, ask him about his caste because here even the Dalits(Untouchable Caste) write surnames like Brahmins. We do not even help the Dalits because they are killing our rights.

"OK, thanks. I'd rather get help from humanitarians than from some progressors like you."

Religious women-1

(A group of religious women talking together.)

First woman- Hey, did you hear about what happened with Rekha yesterday? She was caught in a controversial situation with the priest of the Shiva temple in the neighboring quarter.

Second woman: Yeah, everyone knows about Rekha's affair with the priest.

The third woman- Yeah, Rekha's husband is often away on tour. She must have felt lonely. It may be possible to fulfill her biological needs she goes to the priest.

The fourth woman- I heard that Rekha had invited the priest to her house herself.

Fifth woman : You sound jealous of Rekha.

Sixth woman : We're not jealous, just feel sorry for her. She got caught and we never did.

Religious women -2

(A group of religious women are talking together)

First woman : Do you know which caste the new family in our colony belongs to?

Second woman : Why does their caste matter to you?

First woman : It's been six months since they moved in, and the woman hasn't been seen at the Shiva temple on any Shravan Monday.

Third woman : Maybe they are Muslims or Christians.

Fourth woman : No, they are Hindus. The woman wears a bindi and vermillion.

Fifth woman : May be the woman is Hindu and her husband is Muslim.

Sixth woman : I think they belong to a Dalit caste, that's why they don't socialize much.

Seventh woman : No, I heard that when Sunita's husband fell ill, they took him to the hospital in an emergency and helped with money. They are very helpful and religious people.

First woman : That doesn't make them religious. Unless they come to the temple and participate in religious activities, they can't be considered religious, right?

Everyone in a chorus : " Yes, that's right."

The most dangerous animal

Teacher : Children, today we will learn about dangerous animals. You must be familiar with many animals. I will ask you questions about dangerous animals. Mahesh, can you tell me which animal is the most dangerous?

Mahesh: The lion is the most dangerous animal because it kills and eats many other animals, and sometimes even humans.

Teacher: Okay. Ramesh, can you tell me about another dangerous animal?

Ramesh: The bear is the most dangerous animal. It attacks humans and can tear them to pieces.

Teacher: Good. There are many other dangerous animals as well. Salim, can you tell me about another dangerous animal?

Salim: Sir, the cow is the most dangerous animal.

At this answer, all the children in the class, including the teacher, started laughing. The teacher laughingly says, "Salim, how can a cow be dangerous? Cows are very gentle."

Salim: Sir, my mother tells us that our father was beaten to death by people on suspicion of carrying beef. That's why we had to leave our home and settle in this slum area. So, according to me, the cow is the most dangerous animal.

*Cows are considered sacred in Hinduism and their flesh is not consumed or permitted to be consumed

Politics

I remember there was a pond near my house with a good elevation ridge. On the pond side, just above the water, there were snake holes.

A friend of mine would tie a dead fish or frog to a thread and dangle it in front of the snake holes. When the snakes came out to eat, my friend would throw stones at them and injure them. The injured snakes would retreat into their holes and in greed, they come out again. He would repeat this process until he got tired.

Once, he tried to do the same thing with dogs by using stale chapati and stick, but they bit him and he had to get fourteen injections in the stomach. Since then, he has stopped playing such tricks.

Strong

A believer and an atheist leave the neighboring house in a car. The believer, who is a businessman, is car and honks the horn to wake up the bitch, meanwhile, he gets a call from someone regarding his business and he gets engaged in the phone and in the process car runs over the bitch. The bitch dies right there. The atheist becomes sad after seeing this heart-touching scene. On the other hand, the businessman is still busy on his phone, even though he has realized that the bitch is dead.

After some time, his conversation on the phone stops. He increases the speed of the car. Later he asks the atheist sitting next to him why he is looking sad. To this he replies – Yaar, I am not feeling good because a bitch died after being hit by our car. On this the believer says, hey yaar, these dogs are meant to die. Why do these animals sit on the road? If they sit in the middle of the road they will surely die. You are a very weak-hearted person. A man should be strong like me. Once when I was returning after visiting a temple, I saw that two cars had collided and some of their passengers were dead and some were in pain. I was not distracted at all. I diverted my attention from there and moved the car forward at a very high speed.

Atheist: Without helping the passengers or if nothing else you could have informed the police but you returned, and now calling yourself strong.

To be strong is to avoid the hassles of the police and not to be affected by the people in pain. Just think, when I was not sentimental about humans, it was just a bitch and then this is not the first time that something like this has happened. Come on yaar forget it.

But yaar, her puppies were trying to wake her up, that scene is disturbing me a lot.

Believer- Leave it, yaar. I will put one more incense stick in front of God, may that bitch's soul rest in peace heh...heh...heh...

Pandemic

Champakavan Jungle was under the rule of jackals. Heron had converted everyone into devotees with his meditation skills. Dressed in white, he looked like an ascetic, and he held the status of Rajguru. He often organized meditation camps in the forest, which were broadcast live on an authorized channel called Jungle-Bharati.

The heron always spoke about religion and spirituality, encouraging herbivorous creatures to think positively and maintain goodwill towards other carnivorous creatures, including jackals. Positivity had spread throughout the entire Champakwan jungle.

Vegetarian animals were told that their misdeeds in their previous births had led them to become prey for carnivorous animals. If one eye of an animal was accidentally gone, it would tear out both eyes of the animal. When an outbreak of pandemic occurred in the jungle, the sick animals were left to die, attributing it to their bad luck.

Animals that recovered from the disease on their own were given the status of warriors, and their chest size became fifty-six inches. Under the guise of the epidemic of positivity, the jackals had planned their empire for fifty years.

In the neighboring jungle Nandanvan, there was a lion king who eventually attacked Champakavan. The Jungle Bharati channel kept the animals ignorant of the real situation of the war and continued playing jungle devotional songs. Ultimately, the Champakavan jungle was captured by the neighboring jungle Nandanvan.

Majority

"Since a symbol is needed to focus the mind, I am in favor of idol worship", said one religion, aiming to demonstrate its superiority over the other two religions.

"I am strictly against idol worship, but I am in favor of worshiping the dead, so I am superior", said the second religion.

"I am a staunch opponent of idol worship, but I am in favor of sitting at a particular place and worshiping a particular picture, praying and worshiping it, hence I am superior to both of you", said the third religion.

In a competition to prove superiority, all three of them approached a secular person for a decision and presented their respective sides before him.

The person smiled, thinking that the worship of the symbol was prevalent among all three, but he replied very wisely – The religion is superior where there are more people following it. That is, the superiority of you people if not in your principles but in the majority.

Ascetic

When one of the five dogs, who were following a bitch like an ascetic, realized that he was not going to achieve anything, he went and sat under a banyan tree. At the same time, another dog passing by glared at him and said, "Why have you given up? You are bringing shame to the entire dog community by accepting defeat in this battle. Your behavior is disgraceful."

To this, the dog in the ascetic posture replied, "My dear friend, while following that bitch, I had an epiphany and realized that pursuing lust is not the right path. It leads to moral decline. There must be at leastone dog of good character, and you can see that I am sitting under the banyan tree."

The other dog retorted, "It's not you, it's the banyan tree that's speaking." With that, the dog walked away.

Caste and Status

"Friend, I read in the newspaper today that a Tempo collided with a truck while trying to overtake a car, and all the passengers, including the Tempo driver, died on the spot", one friend said to another.

"Anyone who tries to surpass their caste and status meets the same fate in our country", the second friend replied dispassionately

A Shrewd Ruler

Due to poor governance, there was widespread dissatisfaction among the people. Rebellions were being organized in various places, with police posts being set on fire. Even the intellectual class, which had previously remained neutral, was now openly involved.

Troubled by the situation, the king sought advice from his trusted advisor, Rajguru. Following Rajguru's counsel, the king ordered his spies to place beef in all the temples, pork in the Gurudwaras and mosques, and to kill a few Christian priests and assault nuns.

Additionally, he instructed that all issues should be raised for debate among the intellectual class.

The king's orders were carried out as instructed. The intellectual class became embroiled in debates, while the people of the kingdom began fighting and dying among themselves. This king's name went down in history as a shrewd ruler.

Predictions

He flipped through the pages of the palmistry book, He carefully studied the various palm designs and took note of the favorable outcomes. Upon examining his palm, he discovered that it closely resembled the one associated with positive results, which made him happy.

Mahatma Gandhi's Goat

The goat, caught in the wolf's grasp, begged the wolf by bleating, "I am the goat of Mahatma Gandhi, the Father of the Nation. Even the lion, the king of the jungle, respects me. Please let me go."

"If that's true then I cannot let you go because I was Godse in my past life. And by the way, before you die you should know that these days it's not the lion who rules the jungle, but its we." With that, the wolf sank his teeth into the goat's neck.

*Mahatma Gandhi had a goat Nirmala.

Jihad

"These heretics are so extreme. They have no sense of generosity at all. They are determined to kill in the name of religion."

'Who has forbidden you? You can also become extreme!' "Our religion teaches us to be generous and tolerant."

'These are just excuses for not being extreme. Can you sacrifice your life in the name of religion like them?'

"Why should I sacrifice my life? I am a Brahmin. According to the religious scriptures, the Kshatriyas must sacrifice their lives to protect the religion.

'And you ...? You are a Kshatriya, right? What do you say...?'

"These Brahmins have always been using us for their purposes, now we are not going to be foolish."

'You Mr.?'

" I am from the third varna. I don't have time for this religious conflict. If religion becomes a business then it is a different matter.

'And you ...?'

"I am from the Dalit class. Shame on you that you are asking me to sacrifice my life for religion."

(Brahmin, Kshatriy, vaishya and Shudras are the parts of Hindu caste system)

Solution

"That thinker is quickly gaining influence with his radical thoughts. He has even started challenging the monarchy. He is becoming increasingly dangerous for us. We will have to find a way to get rid of him soon," the king said to his advisor.

"Your Majesty, here's what we can do: order all the sculptors of the state to make statues of that thinker, and have those statues installed at all the intersections of the city. We can also promote him as a god among the public and we can start worshiping those statues. After a few days, you will find that the thoughts of that thinker have disappeared, and only his idols are left. The idols will not be able to do us any harm," said the advisor with a wry smile.

...And by doing so, the king saved his monarchy.

Conversion

He provided a full meal to the hungry man and then, as a formality, asked, "Brother, what is your name? Which God do you believe in? What is your religion?"

The person replied, "From today onwards, whatever name you give me that will be my name. You are my God and your religion is my religion."

Now he understood the secret of conversion.

Dalits

"We Hindus are known for our generosity and tolerance, which is why our religion and culture have survived despite numerous attacks."

"We Muslims are willing to sacrifice our lives to defend our religion. One Muslim is equal to ten others, which is why our influence is so widespread."

"We are Sikhs. Our origins lie in protecting Hindu culture from Muslim influence. However, we are not Hindus. Our bravery is well recognized."

"We Christians are known for our wisdom. We embrace Dalits in our religion and teach them to live with dignity. With our intelligence, we have had a significant impact on the world.

What can we say...? We are simply Dalits."

Tit for tat

I will not acknowledge you no matter how talented or successful you are because you are from the Dalit caste.

What makes you think you can challenge my existence? I don't need recognition from you.

I am not from the Dalit caste and that is my biggest qualification. People like me have the birthright not to recognize Dalits.

From today onwards, I refuse to recognize you. That's it.

Opium

I once came across a quote by a wise man advising people to contemplate deeply on any topic and develop their perspective. I decided to apply this advice to the topic of religion. I studied various religious texts, reflected deeply on them, and then shared my interpretations with others.

Surprisingly, people from all religious backgrounds have united to condemn me to death.

Before I die, I want to emphasize the quote to contemplate deeply on any topic and develop their perspective, except for religion.

Convenient

I said, "Our country is amazing".

He responded, "Okay."

I continued, "Our culture is fantastic."

He again said, "Okay."

"Stones are also worshipped here", I said with great excitement. "In your place, only stones are worshipped," he said.

I was unable to say anything further.

An Empty Mind

All four of us were friends, each following a different religion. One day, we decided to seek the presence of God and we all began to worship according to the practices of our respective religions.

We even put off our important tasks. After a few days, we were amazed to find that each of us had a different deity appear to us, saying, "Child, an empty mind is either the abode of the devil or of God."

After this experience, we returned to our work.

Message

I perished in a religious riot. Upon arrival in the afterlife, my life was reviewed and I was condemned to hell for my disbelief in God and for promoting atheism in my writings.

In hell, I discovered that people from all religious backgrounds who had died in religious conflicts on Earth were gathered for a conference. I took part in this interfaith conference.

The conference unanimously agreed to send a message to the people of Earth, urging them to embrace religionless.

Genies

It was a time of darkness. People lived in close-knit communities, hunted together, and shared meals. The devil, envious of the unity and virtues of humanity, sought to sow discord among them. He created genies, which he called religions, and sealed them in bottles before scattering them in the dense forest.

The following day, hunters stumbled upon the bottles and divided them among themselves. Eager to see what was inside, they opened the bottles. The genies released and entered into the men. Since that day, the men have been divided into different religious groups, often fighting against each other.

Communal

Pankaj's Christian neighbor had a beautiful garden in the courtyard of his house. He had planted many varieties of flowers in the garden, which he loved very much. One day, he told Pankaj that he was unable to wake up early in the morning because he returned home late from work at night, and he suspected that someone was stealing flowers from his garden. He asked Pankaj to keep an eye out for the flower thief.

The very next day, at four in the morning, Pankaj witnessed a person stealing flowers. He scolded him and asked, " How can you pluck flowers without permission? I believe you do this every day." In response, the person turned and shouted, "Jai Shri Ram Bhaiya." He then explained that they offer flowers for worship and it is not considered theft. He then left with arrogance, shouting "Jai Shri Ram" once again.

This incident sparked a communal feeling in Pankaj, and he told the flower thief to pluck as many flowers as he wanted every day. Pankaj also shouted "Jai Shri Ram" loudly.

Nationalist

Hey, every time I hear you talking about social and religious harmony as well as equality. A person should adhere strictly to his social and religious norms, otherwise, our religion and society will be at risk."

"Brother, the fabric of our nation requires us to prioritize social and religious harmony alongside equality. We have a large population of Dalits and minorities, and if they do not receive social and religious protection, there is a risk of violence and even civil war. A nation cannot function without social and religious harmony."

"Friend, you are truly secular."

"Yes, I am."

"Listen, we are staunch nationalists. For us, secularism is an insult. Just like calling someone a whore is an insult, we refer to secular people as whoremaster."

"This is a much-debated topic. Come on, let's go to the coffee house across the street and discuss this topic in comfort."

"Sorry, I don't have any spare time. I just received a message on WhatsApp about salt shortage in the city. I need to go to the shops and buy all the salt packets, then sell them at a higher price."

National Servant

(On phone)

Hello, are you the president of the nationalist organization?"

'Yes, I am.'

"I am Gopeshwar's mother."

'Ok, then what can I do for you.'

"You know that my son Gopeshwar is deeply committed to your organization, both emotionally and financially. In a way, he has left home. After joining your organization, he even left his studies."

'Yes, I am aware that Gopeshwar is a dedicated national servant.'

"Just when he came home for a few days, we found out that he was suffering from severe blood deficiency. We have admitted him to Life-Line Hospital. He needs three units of blood. Kindly send some national servants to donate blood so that Gopeshwar can get a new life."

'Sorry, we are national servants and we are committed only to serving the nation, not to individuals. We believe in religious nationalism. According to us, blood donation is against religion. We believe that by donating blood one will be born anemic, by donating eyes one will be born blind in the next birth and by donating a kidney one will be born with only one kidney in the next birth. We cannot send any of our national servants to donate blood.'

Slavery

Two individuals A and B are seated next to each other on a bus seat, one of whom is educated and the other is a nationalist. It's a long-distance bus, and both have booked their seats online. The bus operator has deceived all the passengers. When booking online, a picture of a Volvo sleeper bus was displayed, and the money was also paid for a Volvo sleeper. Upon reaching the boarding point, it was discovered that it was a bus with very few seats and not a single sleeper. It's nighttime, and both of them, along with the other passengers, have been swindled. The educated person is muttering, while the nationalist is sitting quietly. The entire bus has been deceived, but no one is speaking up.

A- I am currently filing an online complaint against this bus operator with the transport department from my mobile. I will reclaim all my ticket money from these scammers. If necessary, I will take this matter to the consumer forum.

B- Forget it, friend. This happens frequently. I'm so upset that I've already paid an extra Rs 100 to open the trunk to store my suitcase. This has happened to everyone here, but everyone is keeping quiet.

A- It's not about the money. It's about fraud and deceit. I've already filed my complaint online through my mobile while sitting here.

B- Hey, everything's okay. This is just how things are. We should just accept the system quietly.

A- Why should we accept it? It was advertised as a non-stop bus when I booked, but I saw the conductor picking up people along the way. The luxury bus has turned into a local bus.

B- If the driver-conductor is making a little extra money by making passengers sit in the aisle, what's the harm in that? Consider it a blessing that they're not asking us to give up our seats, otherwise, they could do that too.

A- If this system is right, then what was wrong with the British system?

B- You're taking this too far, brother. Our people are our own, brother.

Man

"You should visit the ashram at such and such place."

'Yes, I used to go there at first, but then I stopped.'

"Why? Why did you stop going?

'Actually, I felt a change in myself after visiting there.'

"What kind of change was happening?"

'Well, the bad qualities in me were fading away and I was developing more saintly tendencies.'

"Hey, that's a great thing that you were developing more saintly tendencies."

'No, not at all. What is the point of being a man if you don't have thoughts of bastardy?'

"Yes, that's true."

System

Two people, A and B, are sitting next to each other in a crowded bus. Some women are standing and one of them is complaining to the conductor about the overcrowding. The conductor responds bluntly, telling the women that if they want better conditions, they should take a taxi. He also threatened to drop passengers off mid-journey. The bus falls silent after the conductor's threat. A and B start a conversation about the situation.

A: This is a tough situation. The conductor is making it difficult for all the passengers, even the women who have to stand.

B: That's just how it is. If those who are standing to get a seat, they won't care about the others

A: But it's not right. The women should at least get seats.

B: Everything is wrong. It's wrong to pack so many people in the bus during the pandemic, wrong for passengers not to wear masks, wrong for people to board when the bus is already full, wrong for the conductor not to issue tickets, wrong for the conductor to threaten to drop passengers off mid-journey and wrong for you to not show any sympathy towards the women by giving up your seat.

A: Haha, forget it. The whole system is messed up.

Ramrajya

"Women are treated as objects of ridicule here. They can be used and discarded at will, with false accusations being used to justify throwing them out of the house."

...and the Dalits and Muslims are not treated well either. No one can speak up here...

So just directly say that you have Ramrajya here.

Convenient-2

"It is well-documented that during the Sultanate and Mughal period, Muslims committed significant atrocities against Hindus. Religious conversions were often forced at sword point, and other unspeakable acts were carried out against the Hindus…."

'Impressive! How did you come to know about this?' "

I have studied the works of renowned historians."

'…Then you must have also come across the theory that the Aryans were invaders, and beef was consumed during the Vedic period.'

"I'm sorry, but I have only focused on the books written by those historians who wrote the history of medieval India."

Brahmin

He used to be a Dalit professor and is now retired, spending his time doing social service as a hobby. He has set aside his maid's utensils and has kept a broken cup of tea separately for the street sweeper. He is considered to be of a Brahmin cult among the Dalits, and is saluted by all Dalits of them.

Ash

Republic Day is being celebrated at a government office. The flag has been saluted and everyone is happy. Laddus are going to be distributed soon. The responsibility of purchasing laddus has been given to a Brahmin. Due to performing religious rituals in officers' homes he was promoted out of turn from a peon to a clerk.

Brahmin Maharaj is going to everyone carrying a box of laddus and saying, "Take the laddus with your hand." After reaching me, he picks up the laddu with his hand and gives it to me. Similarly, he starts giving it to a cobbler caste employee also standing next to me by picking it up with his hand. The cobbler caste employee was insistent that he would put his hand in the box and pick up the laddu. Brahmin also becomes insistent that a cobbler can't touch the box of laddu. The cobbler now starts abusing him. The office boss is asking the other Dalit employees not to escalate the issue, and the cobbler caste employee should be told not to make this a matter of untouchability.

After this, all the Dalit employees pacify the cobbler by convincing him, and Republic Day is celebrated with rhetoric like equality, brotherhood, etc.

...This is such an ash, which is smoldering from within

Sevakpur

The country had a long-standing system of monarchy, but the king had become extremely unpopular. The winds of democracy were sweeping through neighboring countries, and the people of that country also desired to embrace democracy. They were actively working to create an environment conducive to revolution.

The troubled king consulted Rajguru. Following Rajguru's counsel, the king declared himself the servant(Sevak) of the people. The royal courtiers were transformed into government servants, the existing social workers became NGOs, and the businessmen, who had been exploiting the people, also started referring to themselves as sevak (servants).

Among the common people, various types of " sevak (servants)" emerged. Some identified themselves as Gausevak (cow servants), while others as Kaar sevak. The more affluent a person was, the more grandiose their title of "sevak (servant)."

In this manner, a democratic monarchy was established in the state, and in response to public sentiment, the country was named Sevakpur.

Bankrupt

During my childhood, I often saw a mentally ill man wandering the streets. He would beg for food and money from people. One day, he sat on the platform of a shop in the middle of the market and started shouting at people. After a while, he calmed down. People would gather around to watch him out of curiosity. This became a daily occurrence, and the shopkeeper's sales started to increase. The shopkeeper even started promoting the man, calling him a deity man. However, the man's madness escalated, and he began kicking people. A rumor spread that the person he kicked would receive their desired outcome. This led to a crowd of people gathering to be kicked and abused. Nearby shopkeepers were pleased because of the increasing sales.

One day, the man suddenly died. There was a dispute between Hindus and Muslims over whether he referred to himself as *'Ammi'* or *'Maa'* before dying. Since there was a majority of Muslims in the area, a mausoleum (Mazar) was built for him.

Whenever I pass by that mausoleum (Mazar), I can't help but feel that it symbolizes the moral bankruptcy of the people, and I involuntarily bow my head.

A Leader Country

The people of that nation were manipulated into becoming fanatics through a conspiracy. They would abandon their work, close their eyes, clap like eunuchs, and dance to a strange tune they called bhajan.

The ruler of that nation regularly fueled fanaticism among the populace. In that country, raised hands during bhajan were considered as votes. In addition to these traits, the most notable feature of that nation was that it was renowned as a secular country and had become the leader of the whole world.

Bankrupt

Once there were religious riots all over the world, creating a situation akin to civil war and world war. Deafening slogans of *Jai Shri Ram and Allah Ho Akbar* were heard in different places, as people of various religions engaged in bloodshed while praising their respective gods. Religious fanaticism spread throughout the universe, causing God to become unconscious and fall to the earth without incarnating. Armed with religious weapons, people surrounded him and laughed when he claimed to be God, saying he was an impersonator. They attacked and killed him, then set out in search of their respective gods.

Sin

At midnight, a truck driver was speeding down the road when he noticed a cyclist on the left side of the nearby bank. Suddenly, a cow appeared in front of him. He swerved to the left to avoid hitting the cow but ended up hitting the cyclist instead.

The truck driver felt grateful that he had avoided the sin of killing a cow.

*Cows are considered sacred in Hinduism

Jhatka

"Yaar, you're charging double for the chicken chili than the place next door."

"He butchers the chickens Halal, while we with Jhatka." "Yaar

In that case, it makes sense for you to charge more."

*Jhatka and Halal are both methods of slaughtering animals practiced by Hindus and Muslims, respectively. Hindus avoid Halal

Lust

After poisoning the dogs in that area, only one dog survived. With the area now empty, dogs from other areas would roam freely there. The surviving dog would stay on the other side of the boundary wall of an empty house and keep barking at them, but could not muster the courage to come out. During the mating season, another dog following a female dog reached the area. Now the surviving dog was ready to fight with the other dog outside the boundary wall.

Future

There were many armies in that so-called secular country. Hindus had created the Ram Sena (army). Muslims also had a Hussaini Sena (army), while Christians also had a Masihi Sena (army). On the other hand, Sikhs had also formed Nanak Sena(army).

That country kept losing in all the attacks that took place because there were many armies in that country but there was not even a single soldier.

Turnes

In a colony, there lived three dogs. The first one was a little bigger than a puppy, the second was of medium size, and the third was full size.

One day, the smallest dog found a bone and started playing with it. The medium-sized dog noticed and approached him. The small dog, realizing he was in trouble, wagged his tail and started licking the face of the medium-sized dog as if to say, "I brought this bone for you."

The medium-sized dog, considering his options, to kill or to let go decided to let go of him he took the bone for himself. Just then, the full-sized dog arrived on the scene.

Now it was the turn of the medium-sized dog.

God and Satan

The person on the train turned his attention to the seat in front of him and saw a lovely innocent girl sitting there. He felt happy seeing the innocent child and thought that children are the form of God. The girl also smiled, thrilled by the affectionate gaze of the person looking towards her. In this way, a human being and God were sitting face to face.

Seeing a human being and God sitting together, Satan's blood started boiling, and he entered into that person.

Now that human being changed from a human being to a lustful man, and his gaze slowly started moving down from the girl's face.

Seeing this changed form of that man, fear started appearing in God's eyes, and the girl sitting carelessly started adjusting her clothes

Reaction

Yesterday, I became extremely angry with him and began to shout at him. He stood quietly, gazing into my eyes, and continued to smile. This only made me angrier... I lunged and grabbed his collar, but he remained standing and smiling.

Today, I ran into him once more. He is once again gazing into my eyes and smiling, while I am avoiding his gaze and looking to the side.

Ray of Hope

Frustrated with repeated failures, he locked himself in a dark room and lay there, feeling almost defeated and contemplating death. As despair began to consume him, he remained motionless. Suddenly, a ray of light appeared from the small hole, gradually reaching his face and bathing him in its warmth. The feeling of disappointment vanished from his heart, and he felt a renewed sense of happiness and courage. He asked the ray, "Who are you, and how have you filled me with such unprecedented enthusiasm and courage?"

The ray replied, "I am a ray of hope. My existence is within you, and the sun of hope shines brightly within you. I appeared just in time to prevent disaster."

Encouraged by ray's words, he opened the door and felt a surge of enthusiasm from the cold winds outside. He resolved to continue striving for success.

Backlash

He caught the mosquito that had bitten him in his fist and, holding it by its wings, put it over to two red ants nearby. As he watched the mosquito fluttering between the two ants, he felt a sense of satisfaction.

The two ants began to carry the mosquito into their colony and soon encountered two more ants. The mosquito's fluttering became more frantic and the man felt even more pleased. After some time, the ants brought the mosquito closer to their group. For more fun in the mosquito's suffering, he released it from the ants. The mosquito was nearly lifeless. He felt disappointed. In the end, he dropped it to the group of ants.

...Now, a victorious expression appeared on his face.

Conflict

He was seated on the bus, munching on peanuts. As the bus began to move, a woman carrying an infant got on, but because the bus was full, she had to stand.

He thought that people had lost their manners, no one was offering the woman a seat.

Then his inner voice suggested he should stand up and offer his seat to her, but he made excuses to himself, saying that his joints hurt when he stands and that he was worried about pickpocketing because he had a lot of money in his pocket. As the woman looked at him with a pleading expression, he looked away, feeling conflicted. When the woman reached her stop and got off the bus, he tried to justify to himself that he was about to stand up, but she got off before he could.

Now his defeated inner voices stopped,

Twoincidents

Two incidents occurred in the same square. In the first incident, a woman was crying and asking everyone about her lost child. People made insensitive comments, saying that they could give birth to children but could not take care.

In the second incident, a disheveled man was searching through a garbage heap for a 100 rupee note.

Soon, everyone in the square started searching for the notes in the garbage.

Truth

Why do people avoid me? Why am I unsuccessful in every aspect of life? Why am I deceived at every turn? Why are people questioning my character? Why, why?" he asked the mirror.

"You are an impractical person. When you lie, your confidence falters. You trust everyone, and your honesty is still a part of you, but it is causing harm to your life. Despite these negative qualities, you also have one positive quality, and that is your inability to accept the harsh truth. Perhaps this quality is what has kept you going until now," the mirror replied.

"You fool, thinking of yourself as truthful," he said, picking up the mirror and throwing it out.

Treatment

The general compartment of the train was crowded, and the man managed to squeeze inside. He found a person lying on a seat and politely asked him to make some space so that he could sit. The person became angry and refused, so the man remained standing.

At the next station, two engineering students entered the compartment. They lifted the lying man by grabbing his collar and made the people standing nearby sit on that seat.

Now the lying man stood, facing away.

Leaders

Two young jackals were sitting near an old jackal and gossiping. The first jackal said - One day I was walking in the forest alone when suddenly a lion appeared in front of me I attacked him and injured him, and I was about to take his life, but my values stopped me, and I left him in the same condition and moved on.

The second jackal said - One day I also had an encounter with a tiger. I beat him, injured him, and left him half dead. I was just about to deliver the final blow to take his life when my conscience troubled me, and thinking about what I would gain by killing him, I left him like that.

"The way you have used words like value and conscience to make your story meaningful is commendable. I would advise both of you to stand in the next forest elections," the old jackal advised them.

Son

When my son was young, he used to go to a teacher who lived in our colony for tuition. One day, on his way to tuition, he saw a very restless dog dragging himself on the road instead of walking on his feet. My son took pity on him and brought him home. We took good care of him and he became very healthy and strong within three to four years. Since he was a local breed dog, we could not keep him tied up all the time. Once he left home during his mating season and was missing for eight to ten days. When he returned, he was very thin. We took care of him again and fed him nutritious food. He then disappeared for four to five days again. This pattern continued, and I followed him once to find that he was with a bitch about a kilometer away. I thought he would come back again, but even after the entire mating season was over, he did not return. Now he has started living with that bitch.

From now on, we have decided that we will never keep a dog of any breed in the future.

Dogs

I accidentally ended up living in an upscale neighborhood. All the houses in the neighborhood have cars except for mine. The most notable thing about the neighborhood is that everyone has dogs. My five-year-old son has been asking me to buy a car as he knows that there are cheap cars also available in the market. I keep avoiding the topic. He understands and starts insisting on getting a dog. I gave him two puppies of a local breed. He becomes happy. One of the puppies is black and white, and my son named him Jackie, while the other is brown and black, and is called Jimmy. I don't like Jimmy because he doesn't let me pet him and runs away when he sees me. He also doesn't wag his tail and is quarrelsome. After eating his share, he eats Jackie's share too. I'm starting to get irritated with Jimmy. My wife says that dogs should behave like this. Jimmy is a dog, and Jackie is a puppy. We argue about this and fight like dogs and our son keeps looking at us in surprise.

A modern man

He was dressed in a coat and tie and went for a walk in the hot afternoon. While walking, he arrived at the house of an acquaintance. When breakfast was served, he only ate a little and left the rest, despite being very hungry. He also drank only half of the tea. Then he picked up the English newspaper from the nearby stool, flipped through the pages, and left it there. After some time, he noticed a CD player and asked to play classical music. When the music started, he began nodding his head and looking out of the corner of his eyes to gauge the reaction of the people present. He was disappointed to see their expressionless faces, so he became irritated and left to return home.

Do you know who that man is? Perhaps he lives in your neighbourhood or your house or perhaps a modern man who lives within you.

Life

I recall that from the time I became conscious, he was by my side. He was my companion from childhood through adolescence. As I became intoxicated with the fervor of youth, my steps began to falter, but he remained with me. Then, one day, in the throes of youth, I stumbled into a pit. I was certain that my companion would reach out and help me out of the pit, but to my surprise, he stood there smiling at my predicament. I became very angry with him, and somehow managed to climb out of the pit and began to scold him... "Unfaithful, traitor... even after all our time together, you stood there smiling at my plight. I have no use for an unfaithful companion like you. By the way, who are you...?"

"I am life," he replied, still smiling.

Even today, I am journeying with that unfaithful companion. I have become even more enamored with him.

Blind

In a rush to get to the office, he was walking quickly on the sidewalk when he accidentally bumped into a person. Blaming the person for the collision, he began scolding him, saying, "Are you blind? Can't you see where you're going?"

"Please forgive me, sir, my mind was elsewhere... but I am not blind," the man said, fumbling with his cane and dark glasses with trembling hands.

Status

He owned a Pomeranian bitch and would often give her leftover juxtaposition to a stray dog, so the stray dog would frequently be around.

During the mating season, the stray dog would pursue the Pomeranian bitch, and the owner tried to prevent them from mating but was unsuccessful.

Eventually, he stopped feeding the stray dog because it forgot its limit.

Mother

As his wife was being taken on the stretcher for delivery, he took her hand and said, "Yesterday, you were in so much pain from burning your finger while making chapatis that you cried all night. Now you are about to experience a different kind of pain. I am very worried about you."

His wife responded, "I was not mentally prepared for the pain of burning my finger yesterday, but I have been mentally prepared for the pain of childbirth since childhood. There is a difference between the two pains. While one brings sadness, the other brings happiness. Don't worry about me at all."

Practical

Hey, one of my buddies is talented, but he's been struggling to find a job and his financial situation is pretty rough. You could help him out?" a friend asked another friend.

"About how old is he?" the other friend inquired.

"He's around thirty or thirty-one," was the response.

"If he's that old and still hasn't found a job, how talented can he be? And even if he was talented at some point, it's probably faded by now. I don't think I can do much for him in that situation," the established friend replied bluntly.

Patriotism

I think that the fees for all government schools and colleges should be raised to the level of private hospitals. Additionally, the fees for all government hospitals should also be increased to match those of private hospitals. This will make those who exploit the country."

"You seem to be very patriotic. By the way, what do you do?"

"I have been working as a clerk in a government office for the past five years."

"Perhaps you were educated in a private convent school?"

No, I got all my education in government schools and colleges."

"OK! By the way, where do you live?"

"We live in Tarun Nagar."

"Oh, that's an unauthorized slum settlement."

"Yes, it is. Due to technology, all government information is now available online, so there isn't much room for corruption. Otherwise, I would have also left the slum and bought a house in a better area."

"What does your father do?"

"He runs a small paan stall."

"Where is his stall located?"

"It's at the corner of Fokat Para."

"Isn't that the same stall that's encroaching on a government drain?"

"Yes, it is. But why do you keep mentioning encroachment? Are you trying to belittle me?"

"No yaar, why are you getting upset? I was just testing your patriotism in today's India."

Intentions

"What else are you doing these days…?" the questioner inquired.

'Uncle, I am currently unemployed…' he said with guilt, bowing his head and looking at his broken slippers.

"My son is busy with his business... he is earning well..." the questioner said.

'So…? So what do I do…? You deliberately add insult to injury…' he said in a depressed tone.

"That was not my intention." Saying this, a wry smile appeared on the lips of the questioner.

Tommy

"Son, you need to eat well. You've become so thin. I understand that you must be exhausted from studying all day in college, especially with the increased study load in post-graduation.

If you don't like bitter gourd, I've also made your favorite Paneer Bhurji and Matar Pulao for you. I'll pack all the paneer bhurji and eight to ten rotis in your lunchbox, along with the pulao in a separate box. You enjoy your meal with your friends.

Here, take this plate of Bhurji and sit comfortably at the dining table. I'm preparing hot chapatis and bringing them over.

And Mr. why do you have your books and newspapers spread out on the dining table? Quickly clear them and make space for Betu to sit. Also, you haven't polished Betu's shoes yet. Hurry up. And before you leave for the office, make your son's bed and iron his clothes.

I'll heat the leftover chapati from last night for you. There's also plenty of rice left, so I'll warm that up too.

Even our dog Tommy isn't eating properly. Maybe his stomach is upset. Give him some milk and rice.

I'll pack bitter gourd dishes and chapatis in my lunchbox. If there are not enough vegetable dishes, you can eat them with pickles. And with that big belly of yours, you should avoid carrying a lunchbox and eating out at your age.

"Don't worry about me so much. You'll make me emotional; I'll take care of myself as I always do. I'll heat up the night's rotis and rice before heading to the office, just like I've been doing for the past ten to fifteen years.

"You don't want to miss any opportunity to barking."She replied looking at him angrily.

Salute

"Yaar, today I want to salute you wholeheartedly."

"Why?"

"You have made the decision to send both your children to Military School and even arranged for their entrance examinations. Regardless of the outcome, the fact that you have considered this in today's crucial times is commendable."

"Yaar You are my closest friend, so I have no reason to hide anything from you. Until yesterday, I was filled with patriotism and had eagerly planned to send both my children to Military School and eventually into the Army, but today I received a phone call from someone demanding a bribe of sixteen thousand rupees to ensure my children's success."

"It's likely a scam. Unfortunately, these types of fraud are common nowadays. Don't let this discourage you. You should report this to the police. Military Schools would not allow such fraudulent activities."

"Yaar He had detailed information about my children, which made me believe him."

"In today's digital age, data breaches are not uncommon."

"It wouldn't be as concerning if it were any other institution, but the fact that it's related to the army is troubling. Even if I assume that there would be no tampering with the exam papers, the data breach is still a serious issue. I had made a tough decision to send my children to the army during this transitional period, but now I have to reconsider."

Think Positive

First friend (opening a sachet) : Here, have some fennel.

Second friend : No, I've stopped eating fennel.

First friend : Why?

Second friend : I used to eat fennel from the same brand, but the last time I opened a sachet, I found a pin in it. It caused a wound in my mouth, so I stopped eating fennel. I've already filed a complaint with the company, and I'm considering taking this to the consumer forum. I'm a conscious consumer, and this is not just a matter of poor service; it's a serious negligence in food items.

First friend : Yaar, even if a few pins ended up in a few sachets during processing in such a big factory, it's not the end of the world. Let's think positively.

Second friend : Instead of encouraging me, you're discouraging me. Shame on you and your positive thinking.

First friend : I understand your frustration, but in critical times of our country like these, it's important to stay positive. I'm not just your friend; but also your well-wisher. Let's think positively.

Moksha (Salvation)

Most people prefer to have their hair cut and beard trimmed at the same salon. Rakesh was no exception. He had been in the same salon for about fifteen to twenty years.

He noticed that the salon owner had put up a photo of Satya Sai in his shop fifteen to twenty years ago. The owner would only start work after worshipping him.

However, after a few days, the photo of Satya Sai was replaced by Maharishi Mahesh Yogi. Over the years, other spiritual leaders like Kripalu Maharaj, Jayendra Saraswati, Nirmal Baba, Asaram, and Ram-Rahim were also displayed on the walls of that salon.

One evening, when Rakesh stopped at the salon to get a shave, he was surprised to see a calendar with a picture of a girl wearing only a bra and panty, advertising liquor.

The salon owner was drunk. Rakesh casually said to him- Yaar this is wrong that you have replaced such a picture instead of the revered Babas. This is unexpected for me to see this.

The salon owner, in his intoxicated state, stumbled over to the picture and touched the model's panty, replied, "Sir, I have now understood that the path to salvation passes through here."

*All the Babas mentioned have been implicated in crimes related to lust.

Destiny

There was a riot in the city, with the rioters targeting people based on their clothing and setting fire to shops based on their names.

Suddenly, a rioter noticed a cart on the roadside with the sign "Durga Kebab Centre" and a list of non-vegetarian dishes. He quickly informed the other rioters.

The rioters assumed that the cart was intentionally named to insult their gods and goddesses. They began to vandalize the cart.

At the same time, the owner of the cart arrived and pleaded with the rioters, explaining that it was his livelihood and that he was struggling financially.

One of the rioters asked him why he had named his non-vegetarian cart after our goddess Durga.

The owner explained that "Durga" was his surname.

Then the rioter asked what is your name without surname?

Ganesh Shankar, he replied. My full name is Ganesh Shankar Durga.

Why have you named as our god and goddess saying this the rioter accused the owner of disrespecting the gods and beat him along with vandalizing the cart.

Lynching

The crowd surrounded a Muslim man and demanded that he say "Vande Mataram" to prove his loyalty for the country. The Muslim man, in an attempt to save his life, recited the entire Vande Mataram song with full force.

The crowd was stunned as they did not expect him to know the entire song. Even not a single person in that crowd knew any lines other than the words Vande Mataram.

Suddenly, a voice from the crowd exclaimed, "Kill the bastard!" Despite being a Muslim, he spoke Sanskrit.

Afterward, the Muslim individual was lynched by a mob according to the planned agenda.

Nationalist

"Happy New Year in English"

"Thank you, brother. By the way, does every language have a New Year?"

"What do you mean?"

"I mean, is there a Hindi New Year like the English one?"

"I don't know the name of the Hindi New Year, but there is a Hindu New Year."

"By the way, which Samvat is the Hindu New Year?"

"What do I know about Samvat-Vanvat?"

"You must have heard about Vikram and Shaka Samvat?"

Yaar, I am only concerned with one Hindu New Year, which starts from the month of Chaitra."

"Please tell me the names of the months of your Hindu New Year."

"We have forgotten our own culture because of the Western culture?"

"I tell the names of the months of your Hindu New Year...Chaitra, Baisakh, Jeshtha, Asadh, Sawan, Bhado,...Phaag."

(biting his teeth) "- Heh...heh...heh...Bhai, I am just a nationalist, I am not as knowledgeable as you."

*Some extremist individuals in India identify as nationalists and seek to reject all other cultures in the process.

Identification

While wandering around the fair, he suddenly noticed a sign that read: "Meet a talented donkey who can identify a person's religion - Tickets only ten rupees."

Intrigued, he purchased a ticket and entered the area. Inside, a group of the audience was gathered in a huge circle.

In the center of that circle stood a donkey with cloth covers over its eyes. Its master, wearing a black cap, and a khaki short held a stick and continuously waved it around.

The donkey begins to circle around. The master walks, waving his stick. He then asks the donkey, "Can you show me where Sardarji is standing?" The donkey stops near a Sardarji wearing a turban.

Afterwards, the master instructs him to wait by the man who is wearing a net cap, and the donkey stops next to a man wearing a net cap who is Muslim.

This time the master instructs Identify the woman with the cross around her neck, and notice that the donkey stops beside a Christian woman also wearing a cross around her neck.

Finally the master instructs to find a patriotic Hindu. The donkey becomes perplexed and begins circling non-stop. Many onlookers anticipate the donkey will eventually choose someone as a patriotic Hindu, but it continues to circle. The audience, who had been applauding the donkey's every move, now start to make noise.

Suddenly, the donkey stopped near a masked man. The crowd's attention turned to him, and they noticed that he was wearing a T-shirt with a leader's picture, holding a trident and a sword, and wearing a gamchha with a party symbol around his neck.

The crowd erupted into applause once again.

The keen observer realized that the donkey could only see the owner's stick from behind the blindfolds, and would only stop when the stick stopped moving.

This realization led the observer to understand that the true talent lay with the master, who was able to control the donkey with the stick.

*Gamchha - A neckwear accessory typically used to absorb sweat.

Ghanta(Bell)

On February 14th, while celebrating Valentine's Day, he expressed gratitude to his parents for not imposing religious beliefs on him.

He continued to visit temples, shrines, gurudwaras, and churches without hesitation. He had learned in his school's Civics book that India is a secular country.

Initially, he interpreted secularism as respect for all religions but later learned that it meant not favoring any religion.

Despite being an atheist, he was drawn to the musical instruments played in these places.

He was captivated by the beat of the tabla during Shabad Kirtan at the Gurudwara, and he learned to play the tabla himself.

He also learned to play the dhol-manjira after observing people singing qawwali and playing dholak-manjira near the tomb.

By visiting the church, he mastered playing various Western instruments.

Reflecting on his experiences in the temples, he realized that he had only learned to ring bells, which had no practical use in life.

*Dhol-manjira - Playing instruments

Marital

The husband expressed his anger towards his wife, saying that her words felt like daggers to him and that it would have been better if she hadn't talked to him at all.

The wife responded angrily, saying that she also had no interest in talking to him.

This led to a wall of silence between the two.

After some time, the husband's anger subsided and he sat in a corner pretending to read the newspaper while glancing at his wife. Seeing no positive expression on her face, he became restless and started pacing around the room.

Finally, unable to control himself, he expressed his irritation to his wife, accusing her of becoming arrogant and asking why she had stopped talking to him, as her silence troubled him even more.

Evaluation

"The boy may have a small job, but he is a highly talented artist. He excels in various art forms such as sculpture, drawing, photography, literature, and music," the mediator informed the girl's father, hinting at a potential relationship.

"Good! How much does he make from these artistic pursuits?" the girl's father inquired.

"He has chosen to keep art as a hobby and has not pursued it as a profession. Therefore, he does not earn any income from these artistic endeavors," the mediator responded.

"Then why does he pursue art? What's the point of engaging in art that doesn't generate income? ...I believe that making money is the true art, everything else is pointless. I cannot allow my daughter to marry someone in such a situation," the girl's father firmly stated.

Assessment

"Yaar, what are your three boys up to?"

"Well, the first boy managed to become a peon through some connections, and the second one has started a tea shop."

"And the third one?"

" Yaar I am worried about him. He does not do anything, He is always attending literary conferences and seminars.

"So, your third son is a failure, then."

  Yes, yaar, just consider it this way.

Market

I recall that during my childhood, we struggled and were only able to have one meal a day. Our father would withhold our food as a form of punishment for any mistakes we made. The fear of not being able to have even one meal would cause us great distress, and we would do our best to avoid making mistakes.

One day, when I confronted my father about a significant mistake made by my fifteen-year-old son, I warned him sternly, "If you don't rectify your mistake, I will withhold your dinner tonight." To this, my son replied, "No problem, Dad, I'll just use Zomato or Swiggy to order food. If you want, I can order for you as well."

The idea of my son not correcting his mistake and arranging an alternative meal once again filled me with dread.

Theif

A man boarded the sleeper class of the train at 9 pm without a reservation, intending to travel until morning. All the passengers eyed him with suspicion, eagerly waiting for the ticket collector to remove him.

To gain their trust, he began to speak, "Friends if you think I'm just an ordinary man, let me tell you that I am associated with a nationalist organization. I have just completed a twenty-day training camp called 'Infusing Courage for the Security of the Nation'. Even commando training pales in comparison to this camp. We woke up at 4 am every day, ran 15 kilometers, and received training to handle sudden dangers. I stayed away from my family for twenty days in the national interest." His words made the people around him view him as a patriot.

When the ticket collector arrived, he discovered that there were no vacant berths. The man gave the ticket collector two hundred rupees to avoid being removed from the train and settled in the space between two berths.

Around midnight, shouts of "thief, thief, catch, catch" erupted from the train car. The nearby passengers immediately suspected the man and looked towards his place, only to find it empty. This confirmed their belief that he was a thief, and they began to berate him.

Suddenly, the man emerged from under the berth and asked if the thief had been caught. He explained, "As soon as I heard the shouts, I jumped out of fear and hid under the berth." Enraged, the passengers began to beat him, calling him a thief.

Relations

Husband: Hey, you have reserve duty during the elections. You'll have to stay there for two full days. My Langotiya friend lives next door. We've been friends since childhood and even started working together. I'll tell him to prepare hot food for you at his place. You can also stay at his house if you want. His wife is very friendly, and they have two daughters who are also very friendly. Everyone will be happy to meet you. Whenever I go to their house, the daughters come to me saying 'chacha-chacha'. I feel like they are my own daughters.

Wife: You are so strange. You're always ready to accept favors from anyone, anywhere, anytime. You don't even feel a little shy about it. Just imagine, if those people ever come to our house in the future, we'll have to take care of them. Don't pretend to be worried about me. It's better to order food from Zomato or Swiggy than to take favors from others.

Relations

Husband: My colleagues at the office often make comments about our family.

Wife: What do they say?

Husband: They say that despite both of us working, our family is not prosperous, and we are always struggling.

Wife: What did you tell them?

Husband: I proudly told them that I am a progressive man. In our twenty years of marriage, I have never asked about my wife's salary or questioned her spending. I take full responsibility for our family.

Wife: It's good that you can take pride in being progressive. Your colleagues have a negative and narrow-minded mentality. Why do they care about our family's affairs? It's terrible to be surrounded by such people.

Husband: They are my colleagues, and they consider my progressive mindset to be sick and bad. They boast about controlling their wives' earnings. It's a terrible mentality.

Wife (suspiciously) - Are you indirectly threatening me?

Husband: No, I would never do that. After all, I am a progressive man.

Wife: Okay, as long as you're not otherwise...

Radiation

Did you know the Taj Mahal is actually a temple?"

"Well, the Taj Mahal is a beautiful building constructed by Shahjahan for Mumtaz, symbolizing love for the entire world. It can also be considered a tomb."

"It's amazing how much misinformation has been spread by British historians. The minarets in the Taj Mahal are not positioned like those in mosques, which proves that it is not a mosque but a temple. There are many such places all over India...I can name a few."

"Please keep your opinions to yourself. I take pride in my knowledge, which is based on careful study and free from any biased views."

Insecurity

Husband: Hey, what should we do with the cash gift we received in envelopes from our friends and family at our wedding? It's around twenty-five thousand rupees.

Wife: I have an idea. Let's add some more money to it and buy a motorcycle for yourself.

Husband: That's so thoughtful of you, dear. I'm lucky to have you as my wife. Let's go to the showroom tomorrow and get a good motorcycle for less than fifty thousand rupees.

(The next day at the showroom)

Wife: Listen...

Husband: Go ahead.

Wife: I want the motorcycle to be registered in my name only.

Husband (suspiciously): Did your mother call you from your mayka (Parents house)?

Wife (innocently): No, it was actually my cousin sister, the one who wore a pink scarf at our wedding. She just got divorced last month. She suggested that I should buy everything in my own name.

Irresponsible

I don't get along with my husband at all. I'm thinking of divorcing him."

'Why? Is he careless?'

"No"

'So is he a spendthrift?'

"No no "

'Does he have an affair?' "No...not at all."

'So does he mistreat you?'

"Oh no"

'Then?'

"He neither goes to the gym nor to the massage parlor. He never takes me to expensive restaurants. He is also not interested in going to malls or watching movies in theaters. All the houses in the neighborhood have cars, except ours. He says I don't need a car. I can't justify owning a car just for show. He thinks owning a car is unnecessary. How can I spend my entire life with such a man...I shudder just thinking about it."

'Hey, it's a good thing that he doesn't have any unnecessary expenses.'

"Then why did he decide to marry ?"

(...unanswered silence)

Jamaati

(In the living room, the son is watching a program about Corona on TV. The father is sitting on the couch, rubbing tobacco. The father, who recently returned from a trip to Kailash Mansarovar, is now stuck in his son's house in the city due to the sudden lockdown.)

"These sinful Chinese people's eating habits are quite unusual. They make duplicate goods, saale communists. God is punishing them. They are uncultured." Our people are religious. Not even a single hair of ours can be harmed by this Corona-Farona."

'Babuji, this virus has even reached countries like Italy, Spain, and America, many thousands of miles away from China.'

"Arrey beta, these are all filthy sinful countries. They keep eating anything. Their way of life and eating habits are also impure and devoid of values. Everyone will die. Ours is an incarnational world, where more than one God has incarnated.. With the blessings of God, I have also been blessed with a son like Shravan Kumar and a daughter-in- law like Lakshmi."

'Babuji, Corona has reached Kerala and Mumbai.'

"Arrey, this is all a conspiracy of the leftists. Don't you see, when the whole of India was raising slogans of Har-Har, Ghar-Ghar, then these people were sitting with their ears full. And these Mumbai people have also adopted all the Western culture. Every bastard will die."

Son (screaming) - Arrey Babuji, it has even reached our locality in our city. Hundreds of people are affected. All the Kailash Maan Sarovar pilgrims have been found victims. Babuji, you have also just returned from a trip there. Arrey Babuji, you have not left us anywhere. Hey, someone, get them out of the house. Hey Lakshmi you listen, don't come near Babuji. Don't even let children come. Babuji, you go to the hospital and die. At least let us live.

Beta, have faith in God. We are religious and pure vegetarians, and we come from a cultured background. Nothing will happen to us."

"Stop it, Babuji. I will call the ambulance government hospital right now. They will come and take you. Don't come here again. If you survive, go to the village."

Brothel

Hello, I am Munni. Are you Labh Singh, the editor of the Sunday magazine of "Rashtravadi Akhbar"?"

'Yes, please go ahead. I am Labh Singh.'

Yes ,"Jai Hind Sir"

'Jai Hind... Jai Hind... go on'

"I had sent one hundred of my short stories and approximately the same number of poems to you for publication, have you seen them?"

'Yes, I have seen them. Unfortunately, none of the creations meet the standards of our magazine. We are dedicated to publishing quality literature. I was actually about to send a letter of regret. Where are you calling from at this time, By the way ?'

"I'm calling from your master's bedroom..."

'Sorry then, I didn't recognize you. I will arrange for the serial printing of all your works. We are here to help improve your writing... I will completely re-write your writings.'

Judgment

"Maharaj, my Brahmin neighbor feels offended by me. If the practice of untouchability continues, what will happen to your vision of a welfare state? What will happen to the Untouchability Prevention Act?" a Dalit complained to a king of a backward class.

"You are foolish and ignorant. It has been many years since the constitutional system ended in our state, and you are not aware that we have issued an order to revive the extinct tradition of untouchability. Without understanding anything, you are accusing this knowledgeable Brahmin Maharaj," the king scolded.

"As a reward for understanding and implementing the royal decree correctly, this Brahmin Maharaja should be given one hundred gold coins, and this Dalit should be given a hundred lashes for his ignorance," the king ordered.

Opportunists

Rupesh has a native-breed dog named Chaap at his house. He has raised Chaap since he was a puppy, and now Chaap is about four years old. Before Chaap arrived, Rupesh used to feed a dog named Bhuru who lived on their street. Bhuru always felt that Chaap had taken his place and would try to bite him, but he never succeeded. Now that Chaap is young and Bhuru is old, they still growl at each other, but when another dog tries to enter their lane, they work together to chase the intruder away. Bhuru is no longer able to stop intruders on his own. When they chase away intruders, they run together and keep an eye on each other to make sure they are together. Everyone except Rupesh thinks that the two dogs are great friends, but Rupesh knows that they are both opportunists.

Logic

You left your expensive lunchbox in the office yesterday. You really need to be more careful. You seem to be at your wit's end."

"Hey, I forgot, but it's not the end of the world. Why are you so upset? I'll get the lunchbox back today."

"How are you going to take food today?"

"Yaar, there are so many lunchboxes at home, I can take food in any of them."

"Who will wash the lunchbox? I don't have time to wash lunchboxes."

"I'll wash it, or better yet, I'll just take vegetables and chapatis in a plastic wrap."

"You always act like a beggar. Everyone in your family is like this."

"That's not fair. You lost four expensive mobile phones, and I never said anything."

"If I lose four phones, what does it have to do with you? I bought those phones with my own money. I earn my own money, I'm not living off your scraps."

Break-up

(A 50-year-old man falls in love with a 22-year-old girl through social media. The conversation between them reflects the frustrations of the present times)

Girl: Why don't you reply to my messages on WhatsApp these days?

Man: Many times I feel guilty that I have fallen in love with a girl younger than my daughter.

Girl: As a man, you think so much. As a girl, I don't even think that I have fallen in love with a man of my father's age.

Man: You are a new-age girl. Whatever it is, you are very great.

Girl: It's not like that. I think you are not able to understand me properly.

Man: That's why I'm calling you great. Let me tell you one thing, I get a lot of energy from you.

Girl: Yes, I know.

Man: Now that you have become my friend, should I take some liberty?

Girl: You can take complete liberty.

Man: I just wanted to know from you, apart from me, how many other boyfriends do you have?

Girl: Only three.

Man: Three? That's a lot.

 All my friends have at least five each. I am jealous of them.

Girl: Do you find this too much? I am jealous of them.

Man: Can I ask you something personal?

Girl: Yes, ask.

Man: I think you are not a virgin.

Girl: I knew that you would ask this question. Even if I tell you that I am a virgin, you will not believe me. I am not untouched, but I am a virgin.

Man: Whenever you get a chance to establish a physical relationship with your boyfriend, please take advice from me. You will benefit from my experiences. Do you know that there are classes for this in many countries?

Girl: If I say that I do not know about such classes, then I am sure you will send me the link to some porn site.

Man: No, it's not like that. Enjoyment is always two-sided.

Girl: I avoid it. My boyfriend remains angry with me about this and keeps threatening to break up.

Man: The first and last goal of life is to attain happiness. There should be freedom in a relationship, not bondage, only then it become fun.

Girl: All my boyfriends want to use me.

Man: This is not called using or being used. These beautiful moments of life are the capital of our life. You will get happiness only if you give happiness.

Girl: Uncle, today at the beginning of the conversation you said that you feel guilty, so know that there was nothing like that. You were trying to portray yourself as sentimental. Every sentence of yours seems to inspire me to have sex. Your bet on me did not work. I am already breaking up with you. I am blocking you.

Guarantee

Security checks were being conducted at the entrance of a large store in the shopping mall. Ranjan and his wife were both subjected to thorough searches, which left Ranjan feeling humiliated.

This was the first mall in their city, and it had only been open for nine or ten months. Ranjan had never been to this mall before, but his wife had visited many times.

Feeling insulted, Ranjan decided not to enter the shop and told his wife, "I feel very insulted. We shouldn't patronize a shop that starts off with suspicion."

His wife then reassured him, saying that there was no need to feel offended by the search. As a government employee, he frequently visited the ministry for work-related matters and was always searched before entry without any issue.

He was profoundly affected by his wife's statement and responded, "I am a government servant there, and all these shopkeepers here serve the consumers, you see." This made him think of the Consumer Forum's slogan, "Jaago Grahak, Jaago."

Arrey, stop it. You're treating the owners of these expensive shops like your servants. Take a good look at yourself in the mirror. Isn't it amazing that we have free access to all this expensive stuff? You don't even realize the world you live in. And by the way, when you enter a shop, don't bother haggling with the vendors for a rupee or two. It won't work here. With that, his wife had already moved ahead, and he followed, almost pulling her along.

Now the consumer within him was enslaved. As he walked, his mind drifted to the signs displayed in various shops, each with different messages like "Please remove shoes and slippers before entering" or "No guarantees in this fashionable era."

From that day forward, when he enters shops, he leaves his heart and mind outside along with his slippers. In this age of fashion, he no longer even guarantees his wife, who was raised in a market culture.

*Jaago Grahak, Jaago- A slogan for consumer awareness

superstition

Bunty often noticed a man who appeared to be a beggar sitting under a dense Peepal tree near his office with a vermilion stone. Every day during lunchtime, Bunty would go to a nearby cart to have tea.

After a few days, he observed that a maid from a nearby slum, who used to sweep people's houses, started staying with the man. He also noticed a small space under the shed of the house next to the tree. Passersby would offer a few rupees to the vermilion stone, which seemed to bring them joy. After some time, a small temple-like structure was built to cover the stone.

There was also a healthy stray dog that seemed to have a special influence on other dogs. Whenever the dog walked, other dogs would follow him and bark in unison. Even during the mating season, many female dogs used to gather around that temple dog. In the temple, people who made offerings would also feed biscuits to the dog as an offering.

Despite witnessing all of this, Bunty, who was a very religious person, found himself automatically joining his hands as he passed by. He started making offerings at the temple and also the dog.

Comparison

Wife: Look at our front neighbor, he washes his clothes every Sunday. His wife must be so relaxed, and then there's you, who does nothing.

Husband: Well, he's used to it from living in hostels during school and college. I've never had to do my laundry, so I'm not very good at it. That's why we have a maid. She does all the cleaning, and washing.

Wife: You always have an excuse. You can't do anything yourself.

(next day)

Wife: Our adjacent neighbor lives so luxuriously. They go on outings every Sunday.

Husband: I can't drive, and hiring a driver would be expensive. We have a small child, so a car isn't necessary right now. We can get around on a motorcycle.

Wife: You don't know how to enjoy life. They eat out three days a week so his wife doesn't have to cook every day. They have the right idea.

Husband: I can give the maid more money to cook, and if you learn to drive, we can purchase a car also.

Wife: If I drive, what will you do? You're so irresponsible. You never do anything. Do you know our behind neighbor always buys gold jewelry for his wife?

Husband: He's a businessman, and he knows gold is a good investment. We don't have the savings for that. By the way, have you ever seen his wife wearing gold jewelry?

Wife: No, not at all. She always wears imitation jewelry. But she probably wears real jewelry to weddings or any other functions.

A few days later, in the morning the wife of the front neighbor came over in tears and said that her husband was having an affair. He has a concubine. To impress her he buys new clothes every week. I discovered a condom in his pocket once, and since then he has been washing his clothes.

That afternoon, the adjacent neighbor's wife came over crying. She said her husband doesn't do any work on his own, and took all her money and even snatched her ATM card.

That evening, the wife of the neighbor behind came over and shared that her husband kept all the jewelry locked up and had the key. He planned to sell it when the price of gold increased. The jewelry was not meant for wearing, and he even threatened to buy gold biscuits if she persisted. This left her upset as she only had imitation jewelry to wear to events.

Marital

Wife: You eat very quietly. Is the seasoning in the vegetable dish okay ?

Husband: It seems like there's a little less salt in the vegetable dish.

Wife: You always find fault with the food I make. You never do like my cooking.

(A few days later)

Wife: I think I might have put too much salt in the vegetable dish today, but you're not saying anything.

Husband: Yes, the vegetables do taste a bit salty today.

Wife: Just have your meals quietly. I tasted the vegetable dish before serving it to you, and the salt is just fine.

(A few more days later)

Wife: How does the vegetable dish taste today?

Husband: Today I have no sense of taste at all.

Wife: Oh, my God! Let's head to the hospital and have you tested for COVID-19.

Conclusion

In that country, a foreign company won the contract through a global tender to identify encroachments in urban area houses. The company's task was to inform the government about houses built on government land, unauthorized additional construction, illegal water connections from Tullu pumps, and blocked drains in front of houses.

The foreign employee of the company, who was sent out to inspect the houses, discovered a government colony right at the entrance of the city. He observed that all the residents there had illegally occupied land. Each person had encroached to some extent, with some encroaching more than others. They had all installed Tullu pumps on their taps to extract more water and obstructed the drains in front of their homes. Nearly everyone had carried out unauthorized construction work.

Tulsi Chaura has been constructed with maximum encroachment. He saw stray dogs raise their legs and urinate on these squares. If someone's pet dog urinates, it creates a stir. Then he found that most of the area was occupied by a temple. He saw that a small temple had been built in the children's playground and its self-proclaimed priest had taken over the entire ground for his personal use. To ensure that he has control over the entire field, he has built a very big house at one end of the field and a toilet at the other end.

He discovered that the residents of the village near the colony had allowed their domesticated cattle to roam freely on the roads and had built concrete structures over their living areas.

After seeing all this, the employee concluded that corruption is a rite and encroachment is a matter of faith in that country.

*Tulsi- basil, is a holy plant, Hindus worship this plant daily

Thugs

The doorbell of his house rang, and when he opened the door, he found a group of eight to ten people standing there. They explained that they were seeking donations for the construction of a Ram temple. He was an atheist, so he did not contribute to religious causes. He also did not donate to local festivals like Ganeshotsava and Durga festival. The locals were aware of his disbelief, which is why they did not approach him for donations. As the Ram temple had become a national issue, it was not feasible to outrightly reject it. He was aware that these narrow-minded individuals could be easily deceived. An idea struck him suddenly. He simply told lie to them that he had already placed the donated funds in the bank branch designated for collecting donations for the Ram temple. Upon hearing this, one of them demanded proof in a confrontational tone. Now he believed that the situation had reversed. He took the initiative and asked if they were authorized to collect the donation. He mentioned that he would verify their receipt book online. On this, the condition of the people collecting donations deteriorated, but they started to call him a traitor. Soon, a group of angry individuals from other parts of the area began to gather, causing him to feel scared.

He had heard about numerous incidents of mob lynching, but he was not one to easily give up. He raised his hand and addressed the crowd, saying, "Arrey baba, I have already donated five thousand rupees for the Ram temple, but I am willing to contribute an additional ten thousand rupees now." Please hand over all the money you have. I will add ten thousand rupees from my own side and transfer it online right now in front of everyone. As soon as he made this statement, the crowd sensed something fishy and began to disperse.

Truth

In the quest for truth, two young men ventured into the wilderness. As soon as they entered the forest, they heard a voice: "Why are you heading towards the path of renunciation at such a young age? This is not the time to escape from responsibilities."

Looking here and there, the first man said, "My wife is a very cold lady. She is not interested in intercourse, so I am not happy with her. I cannot go to any other women for fear of infamy. I am not satisfied with my life, so I am going to the wilderness in search of truth."

My circumstances are different from his. My wife tells me that I am a cold man. She says I am not an erotic man. Neither of us is satisfied with each other, so I have come here in search of truth," the second man said.

"Each and everything has its truth. Your truth is present in your own home, but you do not know it. Now go back to your homes and face your truths," the voice said with gravity.

On this, both men said together, "It seems that you are a very wise fellow... By the way, who are you?"

"I am the truth of this wilderness," the voice replied.

Calculation

Wife: I do everything for you, but you don't care about me.

Husband: Really? Tell me, what do you do for me?

Wife: I wash your clothes.

Husband: I can hire a housemaid for just three thousand rupees a month for this work.

Wife: I cook for you.

Husband: That's another six thousand rupees a month for a housemaid.

Wife: I am your wife... I give you physical and mental satisfaction in bed at night. (A disappointed voice)

Husband: What you're saying can be readily offered by a woman for twenty thousand rupees a month. I give you one lakh rupees per month. After all the services you provide, I am at a loss of eighty thousand rupees a month. Do you understand?

-

Needs

After a river flooded, the government set up relief camps for the affected villagers and provided all necessary supplies. Officials were strictly instructed to prevent any villagers from leaving the camps. Despite the officials' efforts to care for the villagers, a couple was caught trying to leave the camp one night.

The officers scolded them, asking why they were trying to escape when all their daily needs were being met.

The man innocently replied, "You are providing us with all our daily needs, but what about our physical and biological needs for intimacy?"

Prostitutes

(Four men were talking)

First man - "I used to practice religion A. When my baby fell seriously ill and was on the brink of death, I sought help from various religious sites within my own faith, but there was no improvement. Eventually, I visited a place of worship belonging to religion B, and miraculously my baby recovered. Ever since that day, I have had faith in religion B."

Second man - "I used to practice religion B. After ten years of marriage, my wife was unable to conceive. The women in the neighborhood began gossiping about my wife's fertility issues, and even my friends questioned my virility. I sought help from various religious institutions, including those of religions A and C, but it was only when I visited a place of worship belonging to religion D that my wife finally became pregnant. Since then, my faith has shifted towards religion D."

The third man shared, "I used to practice religion C and had been struggling to find a job for a while. Despite visiting various religious sites, it was only after visiting Religion A that I received a job offer the very next day. As a result, my faith has now shifted towards religion A."

A fourth man - "Stop all of you. Are these your beliefs, or are you like call girls?"

Three (untimely)- "What is the point of following a religion that does not bring us any benefits, sir?"

A fourth man- "Well done! If more people adopted your way of thinking, the world would be like paradise."

Belief

You are a very good man."

"Why would you say that?"

"After three years of marriage, you have never asked me about my past. You really trust me a lot, don't you?"

Yes, I do trust, but my trust is not in you. I believe that if a woman wants to have affairs, no one can stop her. That's why I am always mentally prepared for anything... Do you understand?

Law

In doubt of her character, a man killed his wife in the middle of the market. Many people in the market witnessed this, but he was found innocent by the court because the court did not find any eyewitnesses.

Bankrupted

He respected all religions and greeted "Hindus with "Ram-Ram, Muslims with Salaam, Sikhs with Sat Shri Akal and Christians with Hailto Jesus." This meant he believed in all religions, but mentally bankrupt people who fanatically believed in religion killed him. He was accused of conspiring to bring all religions together.

Net

At a wedding, my friend introduced me to his friends. "Meet Mr Ajay Thakar, Mr Vinay Gupta, Mr Kabir Singh, Mr Sushant Khare,… I inferred their castes from their surnames. As he continued introducing me to his other friends, I continued making assumptions about their castes. After a while, I realized that there were people from different castes present in the entire wedding hall. Both upper castes and lower castes were present, except for mine, which was quite non-existent, "Dalit Caste"

*Dalit- untouchable caste

Custom

Hasn't it been three years since you got married, Bahoo?" The mother-in-law asked, looking at her daughter-in-law's stomach.

Maaji, He doesn't even lay a finger on me." Understanding the implication of her words, the daughter-in-law responded politely.

"I don't want to listen to any excuse. It does not affect your chastity or purity. I want a grandson for our posterity to advance forward by hook or by crook. I may bring your co-wife too. You must know that I was also the second wife of your father-in-law. This is the custom of our family, a woman born only to carry forward the race. The mother-in-law interpreted the definition of a woman in her family.

Pati Parmeshvar

This morning, she got annoyed at a man. The man came close to her and happened to touch her in the rush of the crowd inside the bus. Other passengers who saw this thrashed him, and she even slapped him for this. The man got punished only for touching her mistakenly.

She was being undressed at night, with each piece of clothing slowly removed from her body. Despite it being involuntary, she didn't feel upset. In fact, she appeared content and smiled at the man undressing her, as if he was her husband.

*Pati – Husband ; Parmeshwar - Supreme God ;

In Indian tradition woman should consider her husband God

Hypocrite

A man visited an astrologer and expressed concern about his son falling ill frequently. He requested the astrologer to examine his son's Kundali (Horoscope) and provide a remedy.

Astrologer - Based on your son's Kundali, it is indicated that his mother does not provide proper care for him.

Man: Ok. Nowadays, I am facing a greater loss in my business as well."

Astrologer - "Your wife is responsible for this according to your Kundali. She seems to be a big hurdle in your progress."

Man: There is always a quarrelsome situation at my home. My elder daughter is over twenty-five years old, but she hasn't received a single marriage proposal.

Astrologer: "Sir, your daughter is responsible for this. Actually, she is a Mangalik (inauspicious)."

Man: "It means that only women are responsible for all the bad omens."

Astrologer: "Now what can I say, sir… a man might tell a lie, but the Kundali doesn't."

*According to the Indian astrology, Mars is an ominous planet. A person born under the influence of Mars is supposed to be a Mangalik.

Correlation

In the early stages of civilization, man began worshiping God in his mind. As time passed, he continued to grow. After some years, he established a place of worship in his home, and this growth continued. Over the centuries, internal worship evolved into external worship, and group worship became common. Many temples, mosques, churches, and other places of worship were built by man. Unfortunately, this growth was interrupted.

Nowadays we see massive religious structures, but the growth of the human mind gradually decreasing. There is a negative correlation between these two.

Hypocrite

Our boss is a well-cultured and gentlemanly person, isn't he? He always addresses me as his daughter. He is just like a saint," a newly appointed girl said to a middle-aged woman colleague.

Don't you know anything about this old man? He is a sensual person. To regain his lost strength and youth, he took some medicines and drugs, and because of their reaction, he became impotent. Since then, he has addressed all women as daughters. Many cases have been registered against him for provocative acts in different police stations," the middle-aged woman exposed the truth about the so-called saint.

Flight

The little girl closed her eyes in delight, feeling two wings sprout from her body. With their help, she soared higher and higher in the sky, filled with joy. However, her happiness was short-lived as a hawk swooped down, snatched her wings, and flew off. Startled, she opened her eyes.

During all this time, an era had passed. The little girl had grown into a woman, and the hawk-like society had clipped her wings.

Defeat

At night, a man wanted to impress his newly married wife with his intellect, but she continued to smile. He then tried to impress her by showing his prosperity, but she still smiled. When he boasted about his physical strength, she continued to smile. The man nodded in a gay mood and started to laugh. Suddenly, his wife stopped smiling and told him, "No doubt you have many things, but at night you are incapable of satisfying me." Upon hearing this, his laughter stopped, and he began to feel like a loser. His victory had turned into defeat. Unable to bear his ego, he started beating her black and blue.

Now it was the wife's turn to start crying.

Bazaar (Market)

Mother: These days, tomatoes are very cheap, just two or three rupees per kilogram. Yet, you bought this 100-gram pouch of dry tomato soup for twenty-five rupees. You are such a fool.

Son: I'm not a fool, but sensible. We will consume this when the prices of tomatoes are too high in the market.

Credit

Husband – "Who was that old man you were talking with?"

Wife – "He was our principal. Today I am disciplined, dutiful, and a theorist because of him."

Husband – "So, does that mean all the credit for your spoiled behavior goes to him too?"

Bankrupted

In the midtown, the discourse was ongoing. Swamiji seemed very knowledgeable. During his sermon, Swamiji said, "As a triangle has three angles, in the same way, the spirit meets the almighty.

" The devotees exclaimed, "Wah!"

Swamiji further said, "Just as the moon, sun, and the earth are round, in the same way, God comes to the earth." The devotees again said, "Wah...Wah!"

Encouraged, Swamiji started dancing and said, "As the computer has its own memory, just like the spirit is similar to the television." The devotees were too excited and started dancing with Swami. Suddenly, an ambulance from a mental institution arrived. The doctor and the attendants got down and told the devotees, "This Swamiji is a violent lunatic. We have come here to take him back to the asylum."

"How dare you say our Swamiji is mad!" the crowd of devotees exclaimed and started beating them.

*Swamiji - preacher

Brahmhatya

Jailer to Hangman: "Ajay, you will have to hang a criminal tomorrow at 5:00 AM."

Ajay: "What crime has he committed, officer?"

Jailer: "He raped a minor girl and murdered her, that's why he is being punished with this severe penalty."

Ajay: "I will be happy to hang this criminal. If I had the power to judge, I would have hanged him today instead of tomorrow. By the way, what caste does he belong to, sir?"

Jailer: "A criminal does not belong to any caste or religion. A criminal is just a criminal."

Ajay: "I understand that, sir, but he must belong to some caste after all."

Jailer: "Yes, he is a Brahmin. I just saw his file."

Ajay: "Then, I'm sorry, sir... I can't do this. I don't want to be guilty of Brahmahatya. Even though I am a hangman, I may have to face Yamraj in my afterlife. Please arrange for another hangman."

*According to Hindu tradition, killing a Brahmin is considered the greatest sin (Brahmanhatya);

Yamraj is the God of death.

Illegal Faith

Ustad - Jamura!

Jamura - Yes, Ustad!

Ustad - I am worried about this country.

Jamura - Why, Ustad?

Ustad - On every street and square, different religious worship sites have been growing like mushrooms. A few days later, the men will disappear, and these Gods will remain... that's what I am worried about.

Jamura - Take it easy, Ustad. There are so many leaders in the country to worry about.

Ustad - These leaders are also the reason to worry. Meanwhile, have you seen a temple that is built in the middle of the square?

Jamura - I have, Ustad... I even offered a coconut there.

Ustad - Abe your offering has become illegal because that temple is built on illegal land by encroachment.

Jamura - What are you saying, Ustad? You are hurting people's sentiments and provoking communal riots with this.

Ustad - Abe the rights of hurting religious sentiments and provoking riots are reserved for either the big leaders or the big writers. We are slum dogs, so we are not capable of doing this. Understand?

Jamura - Yes, Ustad.

Conviction

Jamura: Ustad, last night I watched the Ganesh Visarjan.

Ustad: Beta, I know about your character. You often get involved in provocation acts or pickpocketing in the crowd.

Jamura: No, Ustad, these days I am leading a serious life and taking an interest in religious activities. I am even watching religious channels. But Ustad, after ten days of worship, people immerse the statue. It makes me feel sad.

Ustad: Relax, this is a tradition. Those statues are immersed after being worshipped. In other words, they are worshipped to be immersed. Those who enjoy worship should be prepared for immersion. Don't be sad. This is a matter of faith, not logic.

Jamura: Ustad, now you are preaching to me.

Ustad: Actually, I am considering a change in occupation.

Democracy

Elections were about to be held in Champakvan Jungle. A tiger and a lion were the main rivals. A leopard was the candidate of the third party. Wolves had their separate regional party and were complaining of exploitation, while jackals had formed their Dalit party. Wild dogs were independent candidates. Deer were the voters, and all the candidates were emphasizing the importance of voting.

Champakvan Jungle was known as a fully democratic jungle among all jungles.

Status

A Dalit boy said to his friend, "Yaar, it's true that we are Dalits, but we have connections with high-class people. Brahmins also come to us and we eat together. You must see this in the evening, I will have dinner with a Brahmin Bhauji in the same plate."

The next day...

"Did you see, we were eating together in the same plate?"

"Stupid, I observed closely. Your Brahmin Bhauji only ate fried food with you, but when it came to rice, lentils, and vegetables, she started eating with her son... I see what your social status is."

Conspiracy

In an underdeveloped and so-called democratic country, the government often blames foreign entities for various mishaps. Whether it's the bird flu, swine flu, border attacks, or even the discovery of human bones in popular Ayurvedic medicine, the government is quick to point fingers at foreign involvement. They claim that primary investigations show evidence of foreign interference in these incidents.

Recently, when Dalits in the country protested against the caste system (Varna Vyavastha), and the government persuaded the main leaders of the movement to believe that the system was a result of foreign influence. They suggested that the caste system was inspired by apartheid systems in other countries, and that foreign hands were behind its existence.

They convinced Dalit leaders back to their communities to spread this message, leading many to believe in the government's conspiracy theories.

Views

A man was sitting in front of Vijay. He was afraid of him. He looked like a monster with two big horns and massive nails on his hands. Vijay was perspiring due to the monster-like man; he wanted to kill him because it seemed if he didn't kill him, he would be killed by the monster-like man.

You will be surprised to know that, until yesterday, both were fast friends because Vijay and Vikram (the monster) were followers of the same religion. But today, Vikram has left his religion and changed his name from Vikram to Akram.

Gods of riots

In a communal riot-affected area, a frightened family hid in a house. As a group of Hindu rioters walked past the house, they shouted "Jai Shri Ram." A child from the family asked his father, "Papa, who is this Ram?" The father was about to explain when a group of Muslim rioters passed by, shouting "Allah Hoo Akbar." The child asked again, "Papa, who is this Allah?" The father scolded the child, but the child innocently said, "Papa, why are you getting annoyed? I know very well that these two are the gods of riots, and that's why we are hiding in this house out of fear."

Gandhi-Jayanti

Instructions had been received from the government to a municipal corporation regarding the celebration of Gandhi Jayanti. A meeting was being held for this purpose. An Anglo-Indian corporator suggested, "We must celebrate Gandhi Jayanti with pomp and show." Another corporator taunted, "Yes, brother, why not ? After all, Gandhi was a friend of the British. He served as a safety valve for the British."

To diffuse the tension, an industrialist corporator remarked, "Mahatma Gandhi was truly a great man, so we should refrain from making negative comments about him." Another corporator retorted, "Yes, brother, you must say that because Gandhiji was a supporter of industrialists. Everyone knows he was closely associated with a prominent industrialist of that era. He was essentially a capitalist."

As the noise in the meeting escalated, Muslim corporators criticized the use of "Vaishnav Jan To Tene Kahiye" (Gandhiji's favorite prayer) and "Hey Ram," considering them communal slogans and labelling Gandhi as a communal leader. Hindu corporators accused him of being a broker for Pakistan and held him responsible for the partition. Dalit corporators claimed that Gandhi was merely putting on a show to address untouchability and criticized the term "Harijan" as an insult.

The situation soon spiraled out of control, prompting the chairman of the meeting to intervene. He urged everyone to quiet down and stated, "We will celebrate Gandhi Jayanti as a formality since we have received government orders to do so."

And the meeting continued.

*Gandhi Jayanti - Birth ceremony of Mahatma Gandhi

Pander

A man to Pandit - Panditji, you have performed all the religious rituals for my daughter's wedding. Along with the worship materials please accept this honorarium of five hundred and one rupees.

Pandit: Do you realize my fee is only five hundred and one rupees?

Man: I apologize, Panditji. Please accept six hundred and one rupees.

Pandit: For just six hundred and one rupees, I wouldn't have travelled such a long distance to have fucked.

Man: Then please tell me your rate, Panditji. How much do you charge?

Pandit: Jajman, I am not a broker for any prostitute or pander. Please do not haggle with me.

Man: Panditji, I am not calling you a pander, but you are referring to yourself as one.

*Pandit - Hindu priest ; Yajman - Host

Donations

"Hi, guys! Why are you crowding at my door?"

"We need a donation for the Ganesha festival." (Rude voice)

"Are you begging for a donation or charging a penalty on me?"

"Take it as you understand."

"How much to pay?"

"Whatever is your belief."

"Even though I don't believe it, still keep these 51 rupees."

"We only issue receipts for amounts of Rs 501 or more.."

"Then keep it without the receipt."

"We are not asking for alms."

"Here, take these five hundred and one rupees. In our country, except for Hindu Gods all other Gods are afraid of a crowd."

Status

While addressing the Gram Sabha meeting, the Dalit Tehsildar was very confident. During the meeting, he saw all members of the Gram Sabha sitting on the carpet, but a man sat separately in the corner of the hall. He asked him, "Why are you sitting separately? Come on to the carpet and sit with others," the Tehsildar said. On this, all villagers started to say, "Sir, you please go on with your duty." He could not understand what the matter was. This event pinched him. After a few moments, he knew that since the lone man belonged to a Dalit caste, he was not entitled to sit with other villagers of higher castes, even though his own son was a Tehsildar in another district.

Knowing this, the Dalit Tehsildar started feeling that his self-confidence was suddenly waning!

*Gram Sabha - Village Voters Assembly ; Tehsildar - Administrator of a Revenue collection unit-Tehsil

Revolution

Ahmed read the newspaper daily while sitting on his balcony. There was a landfill where the colony threw garbage and sometimes food waste too. He often saw healthy stray dogs poking their noses into it, searching for something to eat. Cows watched from a distance as the dogs barked at them fiercely.

One day, Ahmed saw a very healthy bull arrive and take over the landfill. The dogs barked at him fiercely, but the bull was unfazed. Despite the dogs' efforts, the bull remained unaffected. Eventually, the bull became agitated and attacked the dogs with his horns. The dogs found themselves in a position of surrender, their barking turning into howling. Nowadays, it is common for cows and bulls to take over the landfill, while the dogs watch from a distance.

Laughter

To overcome his sadness, Mohit went to a psychiatrist. He noticed that the psychiatrist was also feeling down. The psychiatrist advised Mohit, "Laughing is good for your health, you should laugh for at least two hours daily." He also suggested that Mohit should join a laughter club.

The next day, Mohit went in search of a laughter club and found one. He observed that contractors, leaders, and many other anti-social elements were trying to laugh their best. Even alleged intellectuals were present, but their laughter seemed artificial, much like their lives.

Upon seeing this, Mohit burst into genuine laughter unlike the artificial laughter of the other as he belonged to the Dalit community.

Democracy

The people of the country were frightened by the royal constitution and were fully prepared for a revolution. The royal detectives informed the king about the impending revolution, and the king sought advice from the Rajguru regarding this report. The Rajguru was already aware that the people desired democracy. Following the Rajguru's advice, the king changed his appearance. He set aside his crown and royal robes, opting instead for Khadi (handloom) clothes and a Gandhi cap on his head. He declared himself a public servant and adopted a very polite demeanor. Witnessing these drastic changes in their king, the people were very pleased and requested him to continue in his new role.

The king referred to himself as the prime minister, the royal court members were appointed as ministers and the royal employees were designated as administrative officers. This transformation brought democracy to the kingdom.

Pind-daan

Panditain : "Listen, our daughter Rekha was saying yesterday that she wants to marry Rakesh."

Pandit : (burst out in anger) "Arrey, Did she get only a Harijan (Dalit) to get married with "?

Panditain : "Oh come on ! He has a good government job and will definitely keep our daughter happy. The most important thing isthat they'll get married in court, so we may save a large sum of money that would be spent. In the future, we may use this money to admit our son Chhotu to medical college or for his marriage."

Pandit : "But what will we say to our society ?"

Panditain : "We'll declare her dead to us and show the society that we are totally disconnected from her. We will make her Pind-daan. By doing this, we'll make a fool of our society very well. To throw dust in society's eyes is not difficult for us, and finally, our daughter will be happy."

Pandit : " You are absolutely right, Panditain".

*Pind- daan - Rituals performed for the peace of a person's soul after his death ;

Pandit - Hindu priest ; Panditain - His wife

Fusion

Thousands of years ago, monkeys lived together lovingly in the Indian jungles. No one among them was considered superior or inferior. All monkeys were equal. Criminal-minded monkeys were punished with exile. They would go to nearby democratic jungles as migrants.

Once, a group of punished monkeys returned to the forest. They wore Gandhi caps and Khadi clothes, looking very attractive. They taught the Indian monkeys a lesson in democracy and proved that democracy is the best ideology and policy. The Indian monkeys then started a democratic movement. During this time, Darwin's theory emerged, and all the monkeys transformed into human beings. Those monkeys who wore Gandhi caps and Khadi clothes became democratic leaders.

Today, they are leading us.

Wisdom

In ancient times, a group prayer was organized to receive blessings of wisdom for all humanity from God from people all over the world. God was pleased and granted blessings of wisdom to all of them. However, after receiving wisdom, some people began to challenge God's existence, causing belief to wane. God realized that His existence was now in jeopardy and foresaw a bleak future. In response, He withdrew His blessings.

Now, fully aware of the situation, God is no longer swayed by any form of prayer and is unwilling to bestow blessings upon them.

Corrigendum

A man had spent his entire youth in penance. As he reached old age, God finally appeared before him and asked, "Tell me, what do you desire as a blessing?"

The old man replied, "I only wish to have a woman now."

God scolded him, saying, "You fool ! You could have easily found a woman in your worldly life, but you wasted your entire life seeking her. You have made a mistake."

The man responded, "Lord, the purpose of my penance was different, but I have realized that one cannot escape the world. I want to correct my mistake and make the rest of my life meaningful."

Ash

To symbolize national unity, an artist crafted a Hindu temple, a mosque, a church, and a Gurudwara into a large wooden staff. Due to the slightly zigzag shape of the staff, the temple and the mosque could not be made in equal size, leading to disputes between them. Eventually, both structures were set on fire in frustration, and the flames spread to the Gurudwara and the church.

After some time, only ash remained, no longer belonging to any of the religious structures. It was simply ash.

Improbity

In front of my home, some street dogs were playing. The dogs, bitches, and puppies were all playing together. They were pulling each other's legs, dashing around, and licking each other. They were stuffing something in their mouth, running fast, returning quickly and then running fast again. I observed them for a long time. Suddenly, I got up and brought out a stale chappati (bread) from my kitchen, and threw it among them.

Now they were quarrelling terribly, and a devilish smile appeared on my lips.

Improbity

Since I was running late, I was walking quickly. When I saw a large crowd, I stopped and noticed two men arguing and shouting at each other while grabbing each other's collars. Like the others around me, I watched the situation escalate dangerously. I feared that one of them might pull out a dagger or even a pistol. I wondered what I would do in that situation - would I try to mediate or would I run away?

As I pondered these thoughts, I suddenly saw the two men release each other and walk away, still hurling insults at each other. The onlookers, disappointed by the anticlimactic end, dispersed and went their separate ways.

I continued on my way, muttering to myself, "Idiots! If you can't fight properly, why bother fighting at all? Your unnecessary drama has wasted my valuable time. I need to get to the office soon."

Slavery

Master : "On your request, I released you, but you have come back to me... why?"

Slave : "Sir, I was released by you, but I could not free myself from my own mentality of slavery. Kindly make me your slave again."

Public interest

During a sting operation, a CD was made by a popular news channel in which a prominent leader of the ruling party was shown accepting a bribe. The ruling party managed the channel and the channel announced that in the public interest the contents of the CD would not be broadcasted .

A few months later, as elections were approaching, the channel came under opposition control and, in the public interest, the CD was broadcasted by the channel.

System

Staring at the big English Mastiff, a puppy growled. The giant English Mastiff calmly sank his teeth into the puppy's neck and killed him instantly.

I was there when this occurred, and since that time, a tail has grown out of my backside that always keeps on wagging.

Captured

(In a store)

Son – Papa! I want this packet of noodles.

Papa – No beta (dear son), this is junk food. You may get sick from eating this.

Son – Mummy, please!

Mummy – No beta, papa is right. This is harmful for your health.

Son – But in the TV commercial, the company says it's nutritious.

Papa – Beta, companies often lie to sell their products.

Son – No, that can't be true. I think both of you are lying to save your money.

Status

(At a stationery shop)

Customer – Brother, please let me have a cheap ballpoint pen.

Shopkeeper – Look at this one. This is a really good and branded pen. You can't find a smoother and better-looking pen like this anywhere and it's only for twenty rupees.

Customer - Brother, I want a very low-priced pen that I can use and throw away and the price should be two or three rupees.

Shopkeeper – Sir, look at this one. This is also a branded pen and the price is not so high, only ten rupees.

Customer – Bro, I've told you earlier that I just want a low-priced pen, the price should be two or three rupees, but you are showing me expensive pens and wasting my time.

Shopkeeper – For your information, we don't sell cheap items here in our store. We only keep quality products as our customers are not of low status.

Customer – It means, I dare not buy a pen from your store because my status is not as high as your customers?

Shopkeeper – It may be.

Insecurity

Miyaan (Brother), why are you collecting chanda (donations) for a Hindu festival? Don't you know that the worship of statues is strictly prohibited in Islam?

Bhaijaan (Dear brother), don't you know that a Muslim was killed by some extremist Hindus on suspicion of eating beef? I just want to say, *"Jaan hai to Jahan hai"* (If there is life, there is the world)

Eunuch

Eunuchs : " Hai-hai Chikane (Hi Handsome), give us money and receive blessings from us. Our blessings are very effective. You will marry a very pretty woman and treat her like a queen."

Man : I was married to a very pretty woman, but she left me for my own friend.

Eunuchs : Then why are you here? Come with us and clap.

Lesson

I remember my memories of childhood when there was a single guy who had a cricket kit in the entire colony. He shared his kit with us in a special condition that he had the opportunity to bat as long as he wanted.

We got tired with bowling and fielding but when he got bored of it, he gave us the opportunity to bat.

Now at every stage of my life I remember my childhood memories, its nostalgic.

Bitter truth

"Really yaar, this era is not for gentility. People consider only a poor fellow to be a gentleman."

'My dear brother, these days only poor fellows are the gentlemen'

Speed

"I saw your race yesterday. After seeing your willpower and dedication to your master, I started thinking that we dogs are nothing in comparison to you", a street dog said to a racing horse near a stable.

"No, brother, this is not true. Willpower and dedication mean nothing to us. Actually, we face a fierce punishment after losing the race; fear is what drives our speed", the horse replied.

Character

Ustad – Jamura !

Jamura - Yes, Ustad !

Ustad - Abe, Who was that woman you were with yesterday? I'm pretty sure she was not your wife.

Jamura - Ustad, she is... but why are you interrogating me about her? Are you doubting my character?

Ustad – Abe ! This is not just my doubt, but my belief that you are a characterless man.

Jamura - Ustad, you are spoiling my character.

Ustad - Abe, Not just me, but the whole world thinks the same. The whole world says you are characterless.

Jamura - How can you say that, Ustad?

Ustad - Abe, Before yesterday, I thought you were a well-cultured man, but last night I saw you without a mask. Beta, this is the tradition of the world – 'a man is considered innocent until proven guilty. Everyone lives in a glass house and throws stones at others, forgetting that every action has a reaction.'

Jamura - So, Ustad, are you also a characterless man? Ustad

- Abe Am I from another world? You lack character.

Jamura - (moaning) What can I do, Ustad? I've been insulted by my own wife many times for no reason.

Ustad - Then why don't you kick her out of the house?

Jamura (Emotionally) - Ustad, I have a child... my own blood, Ustad. I can find another woman in the market, but my own blood, Ustad...

Ustad - So, you are compromising for your son.

Jamura - Ustad, not just me, but the whole world compromises after marriage.

Ustad - You sound like a guru.

Jamura - It's because of the company I keep with you.

*Jamura and Ustad - street players

Honour of needs

Yesterday, I had a conversation with my dear Uma about love being a spiritual connection that does not involve physical intimacy. It is important to honor each other's emotions.

Today, she was found in a controversial situation with a married man and they may face consequences from the community.

It seems that Uma prioritizes physical needs over emotional respect.

Mother

We often gave stale foods to a pregnant street bitch. At the proper time, she delivered puppies. To supply the food to the puppies, she went in search of food here and there and brought eatables for them. I used to observe her. After some week she started coming along with her puppies to us and looked us with hope.

Nowadays her puppies are grown-up and keep on fighting for food in our courtyard and they do not win now their mothers in the courtyard.

World Renewal

He was a reformist who aimed to change the world. To achieve this, he needed to awaken the dormant masses. Initially, he gently nudged them and said kindly, "Please wake up." However, the people remained unmoved. He then shook them vigorously, prompting some reaction before they drifted back to sleep.

He got up and poured a bucket of water upon them. This finally all the people woke up and got him to get asleep forever.

Knowledge Selling

I possess knowledge in various subjects. Every morning, I would gather this knowledge in a sack and carry it on my back to share with those in need. As the act of sharing knowledge increases one's own knowledge, my storage of knowledge grew, and I began distributing it more generously.

One day, I opened my sack in front of a man and began explaining knowledge to him. Suddenly, he became angry and told me to pick up my belongings and leave. I was taken aback by his reaction. I gathered all my knowledge back into the sack and left with a heavy heart. This scenario repeated itself frequently thereafter. People seemed to be afraid of me. Then, my inner voice suggested that it was time to not just distribute knowledge but to sell it. The following day, I started selling knowledge.

Today, my business has expanded globally. Numerous branches of my knowledge have emerged, such as Yoga Guru, Management Guru, and Spiritual Guru, among others.

Defect

Sir, there are too many defective lots rotting in our storehouse. We could start a 'sale' and sell all the defective lots in it. By doing this, we can earn money," a manager advised the owner.

"You have a completely defective mentality. You should know that salespeople shy away from defective materials and customers do the same," the owner replied.

"Through different media channels, we should promote that our products are 100% exported. However, for Gandhi Jayanti, we are offering export-quality clothes at discounted prices. Also, put a photo of Mahatma Gandhi on the small defects and a tricolour flag on the big defects."

Talent Hunt

The king of the kingdom was fond of watching TV programs. One day, an idea struck his mind that he should select his prime minister, cabinet ministers, and royal employees through talent hunt programs. He began preparing for this and sought the help of all the TV channels. To select the ministers, a program called "Laughter Show" was created because the king believed that ministers should be like jesters who can divert the public's attention from problems by making them laugh. For the Prime Minister selection, a program named "Father Of Comedy" was devised and for the royal court members, a program called "Sasti Music Mein Jhoom" was created. This program was based on Raga Darbari and Raga Jaijaivanti, as having an oily tongue was essential to being a member of the royal court. Inspired by IPL cricket, royal employees were acquired through an auction. To promote women's empowerment fifty percent reservation was provided for all positions and programs named "Smart Miss" and "Smart Mrs." were organized to select them.

Through these efforts a new government was established. After a few months, the new government decided to hang the king because apart from the king, everyone else was talented and they deemed the king useless.

Impotent

He was unaware of the sexual relationship and his friends had described it as a heavenly experience. He was curious to experience it himself, driven by his manly ego but his conscience held him back. There was a constant battle between his ego and his moral values.

One day, influenced by his ego, he visited a prostitute intending to prove his manliness. However, his conscience intervened at the last moment, causing him to change his mind and leave. The prostitute insulted him by calling him impotent.

When he shared the incident with his friends, they also mocked him by calling him impotent. After hearing their comments, he started to question his own masculinity and felt like an enlightened impotent.

Taliban

Since America is a Christian nation and Jesus Christ was born in Israel, Indian media shows fanaticism for these two countries and blames America for every mishap. Even for the dissolution of the USSR, Indian media claims that only America is responsible. Only CNN channel shows us real information," said an Indian Christian.

"Indian media provides false news about Kashmir. Only the PTV channel shows us real facts, so despite the ban, I watch PTV," said an Indian Muslim.

"Sorry...both of you are Indians, but you are talking like traitors..." A Hindu interrupted suddenly.

"We don't live in India...Actually, we live in Hindustan, where Hindu Taliban sometimes demolish Babri Masjid and sometimes kill pastors," both the Christian and Muslim replied together.

Dalit

We Hindus are generous and tolerant, which is why our religion and culture have survived to this day," said a Hindu.

"We Muslims are staunch in our beliefs and will do anything to protect our religion, even if it means sacrificing our lives. One Muslim is equal to ten others," a proud Muslim declared.

"We are Sikhs. Our religion was born to protect Hindu culture from Muslim attackers but we are not Hindu. Our bravery is renowned worldwide," a Sikh stated.

"We Christians are wise and believe in equality. We teach self-respect to Dalits who have converted to Christianity. Our wisdom has allowed us to govern all over the world," a Christian remarked.

"Now what can we say? We can only say that we are Dalits," a disappointed Dalit expressed.

*Dalit - untouchable caste

Blackmail

A man to a child: "Hey! Where are you going with this bill book?" Child: "Uncle, we are collecting donations for the Ganesh festival." Man: "But where are your other companions?"

Child: "Uncle, we are going to collect donations door to door separately, with a separate bill book."

Man: "If you work this way, you will never collect enough donations. You should go in a group. People don't donate out of self-inspiration and faith, but out of fear of the crowd."

"As big as the crowd, so big the donations. Understand?"

Compromise

Showing me a dagger, they ordered, "Say loudly, *Allah Hu Akbar*." I did the same without any hesitation because I wanted to reach my colony quickly and show the *Trishul* (trident). I wanted to make others say *"Jai Shri Ram,"* but I knew that would only be possible if I stayed alive. So, I said loudly, "Allah Hu Akbar," without any hesitation.

The biggest religious person

(Two men A & B were talking)

A- "A man should be religious. I am an example myself. I wake up early in the morning daily and go to the Ganga (The Holiest River of India) to take a bath. After coming from there, I worship God for at least two hours. I also fast regularly."

B- "Tell me, how many followers of other religions have you killed?" A- "None."

B - "Then you are not capable of saying that you are a religious man. Look at me...I am an example. In each and every communal riot, I kill a minimum of five to ten followers of other religions. Now tell me, who is more religious… you or me?"

A- 'Brother, you are the most religious person.'

Eunuchs

That day, I asked the group of eunuchs why they didn't do any respectable work. To this question, they replied that they knew nothing except clapping.

In jest, I suggested that they join a religious television channel.

Nowadays, I see them in leading roles on various religious television channels. They clap and dance , the crowd of devotees claps and dances along with them.

Today, I am afraid and worried to imagine that people all over the world are becoming eunuchs.

Pride

He was a Hindu in a Sikh-majority area. He used to go to the Gurudwara daily and also read the Guru Granth Sahib. After Indira Gandhi's murder, during the Hindu-Sikh communal riots, he saved himself by claiming that he believed in Sikhism. After a few years, he was transferred to a Muslim-majority area. There he used to go to the Masjid (Mosque) and read the Quran. After the Babri Masjid destruction, during the Hindu-Muslim communal riots, he claimed to believe in Islam to the Muslim rioters and revealed he was a Hindu by birth to Hindu rioters, thus saving himself.

These days he is posted in a Christian-majority area. He goes to church and reads the Bible daily. He criticizes both Hindus and Muslims for their staunchness, citing references to Pastor's murders and the destruction of churches. He believes he will be able to save himself again.

He proudly states that he is a Hindu, but only in his loneliness.

Adopted Daughter

(Two employees, A & B, were talking.)

A: "Sign on this form."

B: "What type of form is this?"

A: "Actually, the government wants each citizen to adopt at least two poor girls and bear the expenses of their education. Since we are government employees, we should adopt more than two girls. It is our social and moral responsibility too."

A: "Guru, your income generates too much by bribe. If you want, you can adopt several poor girls because you are capable of this, but I dare not do this."

B: "Listen, there are also many young girls on the list." (A whispered voice)

A: "Oh! That's the matter. Why didn't you tell me this first? Let me see the list. I would adopt all the young girls."

Worship

He reached home late at night from a marriage reception. In the morning, his wife gave him a list of worship materials related to her Karvachouth fasting. She warned him to bring all the materials on the list no matter what. Due to his workload in the office and the reception, he forgot to bring the materials. When he entered the bedroom, his wife was lying on the bed. He said to her guiltily, "Sorry darling, I couldn't bring the worship materials this time."

"Oh, come on darling... This is not the time for worthless talks," she replied. She then took his hand, pulled him towards her, and switched off the lamp with her left hand.

*Karvachouth - A worship done for husband's long life

Competition

There was an established and reputed herbal shop in midtown named Agrawalji's Herbal Shop. After some years, four more herbal shops were opened adjacent to it and all of the shopkeepers hung boards in which they quoted the same name. After some months, the established shopkeeper made a change in his board – The Real Agrawalji's Herbal Shop. After some days, the others copied it. Eventually, the established shopkeeper wrote on the board - Raghunandan Lal Agrawalji's Herbal Shop. Taking one step further, other shopkeepers wrote on their boards - The Real Raghunandan Lal Agrawalji's Herbal Shop.

Double Status

A man bought shoes for Rs. eight hundred, but after a fifty per cent discount, he got them for four hundred rupees only. He kept on walking and walking wearing the shoes with the tag of Rs eight hundred. He was approached many times by people, but he did not remove the tag. He wore the shoes until they were torn.

This way, he maintained his double status.

Achievements

(Three women, A, B, and C, were talking.)

Woman A : I like freedom very much. I left my husband too. I don't care for anybody. My freedom is my achievement.

Woman B : I believe in achieving things myself. I have been a meritorious student from the beginning, and today I am a self-dependent woman. This is my biggest achievement. My husband would not help me, so I divorced him.

Woman C : I have been facing mental and physical oppression from the beginning and to this day I am neither a divorcee nor abandoned. This is my biggest achievement.

Bazaar(Market)

(Two men, A & B, were talking)

Friend A : "What's wrong, buddy? It's our Independence Day today and you're wandering around with a long face. We should at least show some patriotism today. Look at me... I've been preparing for four days. First, I went to the market and bought Khadi clothes. Nowadays, Khadi is available in different varieties. This year, I bought a tricoloured shirt for my son. The national flag designs are really trendy now. After buying the clothes, I got tricolored flags for each member of my family and you..."

Friend B : "Sorry, friend. I don't want to comment on the commercialization of nationalism or the nationalism of the market."

Postmortem

In that democratic country, elections were about to be held. A leader of the opposition, who was also a businessman, had been killed. Both the ruling and opposition parties were accepting that it was a political murder. The ruling party claimed that this murder was sponsored by the opposition to create a sympathetic environment, while the opposition alleged that the ruling party killed him out of fear of his popularity among the voters. The late leader's son was also screaming and cursing the ruling party, perhaps indicating his interest in joining politics. Meanwhile, the opposition and other regional parties called for a Bandh on a specific date.

During the Bandh, with deserted roads and shops, a TV reporter sought the opinion of a common man on the event. Fortunately, he found a disillusioned common man. When asked by the reporter, the common man replied in a hopeless voice - "This is definitely a political murder of the people, by the people, and for the people."

It was a different matter that the opinion of the common man was edited by the channel.

True Lover

Looking at the rose, he felt irritated. He always felt that his faithless beloved was emerging from the rose. He wanted to kill her, but it was just his illusion, so he was not capable of doing anything. Finally, he crushed the rose hard, but after a little while, he felt that his inner existence, along with his hands, had become fragrant.

Now he forgot about revenge and had become a true lover.

Auction

Three men, A, B, and C, were living in a village. Mr. A belonged to the high class, B to the middle class, and C belonged to the lower class. All three had taken government loans separately and were declared defaulters. Once the recovery officers went to their village for recovery, they first reached Mr. A's bungalow. Seeing them pulling out the legs of roasted chickens and drinking wine, they said to Mr. A, "Dauji, we will recover money from you anytime... where will the money go?" From there, they went to Mr. C's hut. Seeing his poverty, their eyes watered. They became sentimental and without saying anything to Mr. C, they moved to Mr. B. Upon reaching there, they scolded him and said rudely, "Seeing the money you have, you have become dishonest and are trying to deceive us. Now we will auction your guaranteed land against the loan."

After a little while, the auction procedure started.

Business

In that democratic country, the band was a common occurrence. The band was called for very minor reasons, sometimes by the ruling party and sometimes by the opposition and other regional parties. During the band, shops were forcibly closed and it was announced in newspapers that the market was closed due to self-inspiration.

During the band, a shopkeeper and two laborers asked a small political leader, "What do people gain from the band, apart from losses?"

"Appealing for the band is our political business," he replied with a devilish smile.

Offering

The stolen statue of a goddess from a very old temple was recovered by the police from the thieves. The statue was kept in the police station for the devotees to offer cash and other items. The devotees started making offerings to the goddess. The Thaanedar and his staff also became devotees due to the large offerings. Everyone was happy. Seeing the profits, the Thaanedar wanted the statue to remain in the Thana forever. He prayed for it daily. The statue also felt that in the old temple, no one came to worship it, but now there were many devotees, so it decided to stay in the Thana. Finally, one day the statue said to the Thaanedar – "Tathastu."

After a few months, a temple of Thaneshwaridevi was built by the Thaanedar and the devotees on the Thana premises.

*Thanedaar - In charge of a police station; Tathastu - As you wish

Frustration

The curfew was imposed in a city affected by communal riots. To prevent further unrest, the city was placed under army control. A press reporter sought information on how the army planned to control the riots. He approached the Major and inquired about their strategy.

The Major responded, "If the rioters attempt to cause trouble, we will take strict action against them. If they try to set fire to any property, we will respond even more forcefully. And if they attempt to harm anyone, we will take the most severe action against them."

"Sorry, sir, but your words sound more like those of a politician," the reporter remarked in surprise.

The Major, frustrated, replied, "What else can we do? We are soldiers in a democratic country."

"In such challenging circumstances, it might be better to say, 'We will shoot the rioters,'" the reporter suggested.

"Don't talk nonsense, or we might have to shoot you," the Major responded angrily.

Nervous Breakdown

He formed a big statue with clay. He kept looking at it with gladness. Suddenly, he felt that the statue was smiling. He got frightened and sat down at its feet in a downcast position. Now his happiness disappeared. After a little while, he looked up and found that the statue had grown to a very large size, and he was a dwarf compared to it. Just then, he accepted it as almighty and with an unknown fear, started crying for protection and began daily worship of the statue.

Today, we can see that the statue and the man are dependent on each other everywhere.

Curse

A dog and a goat were standing together when suddenly a child picked up a stone and hit the dog. The dog cursed him- In the future, the child becomes the leader of a staunch religious organization.

The goat asked the dog, "Are you cursing him or a blessing? These days only these types of leaders are in positions without doing anything."

The dog replied, "Actually as I was a religious leader in my past birth."

Manhood

In the court of the dogs, a case was filed against a dog. He was accused of biting his own master.

The judge asked him why he had bitten his own master.

He replied politely, "My lord, I watched the news on television that the flesh of dogs is eaten by people in some countries. Seeing this upset me, and as a protest, I bit my own master." But it was just symbolic.

The judge said, "By doing this, you have sought revenge, which shows courage in a dog. Biting your own master has brought shame to the dog community. This is an unforgivable crime, so you…"

"Sorry, sir, but you are the one showing courage by teaching me the lesson of loyalty after knowing all the facts," the dog interrupted the judge.

"Shut up, you fool! Now listen to my decision – By biting your own master and defaming the dog community and also you have brought contempt to the court. Therefore, you are sentenced to death." The judge punished the dog.

Democracy

After gaining freedom, the country embraced the democratic system. However, after some years, the ruling party began to transform democracy into an imperial system. In response, the opposition resorted to democratic method and in the subsequent elections the voters elected the opposition party. After a few months, people realized that there was little distinction between the two parties. Eventually, the ruling authority was handed over to criminals by the people. This gave all the criminals in the country a license to commit crimes. Frustrated, the voters then elected eunuchs in the next election.

Today, people feel betrayed by all these leaders. Perhaps in the next election, voters may opt for slavery.

Elites

Saheb, please give me some stale food to eat, as I have not eaten anything for two days," a beggar pleaded to a man.

"You lazy fellow...you don't want to do any work, because it is your habit to live on dishonest means...Now get out of here," the man scolded him.

When the beggar went away, the man put stale food before his dog, but the dog was full and only sniffed the food then sat down near it and kept watching. Whenever another dog or hen came to eat the food, they would approach the food and then back off. This happened many times.

In this way, neither the dog ate the food himself nor fed it to others. Observing his behavior, the man murmured, "It seems this dog is fully influenced by me...after all, a full belly master's dog should be full."

Address

Girl: "Sir, you are looking very handsome like a film star." Man: "Oh really? My wife says the same thing."

Girl: "Oh, Brother are you married?"

Man: "Yes, I have a son too."

Girl: "Then, uncle, bye... bye..."

Dignity

Ustad: Jamura, why are you wandering with a long face?

Jamura: Ustad, yesterday I was beaten by the people for provocation acts.

Ustad: Hey, this is a matter of pride, celebrate this.

Jamura: Ustad, in the mid-market, I was insulted by the crowd and you are making fun of me.

Ustad: Hey, do not feel insulted and listen to me - Actually, respect and dignity are mortal things. Only money is the main thing. Your money has not been spent in the police station or hospital… that's it.

Jamura: Ustad, great men, and saints have said that money is a mortal thing. Respect and dignity are immortal things, but you are telling just the opposite. Ustad, I am worried about my impression and you are joking.

Ustad: Hey, I have been telling you for a long time not to watch religious TV channels, but you ignored my advice and stored the garbage of respect and dignity into your mind. Meanwhile, listen -

respect and dignity are illusions of the mind. You should not feel humiliated and know one more fact, that no one's impression is good in the whole world. Even your great men and saints are also in fame.

Jamura: Ustad, it's wrong that you are creating a bad image of our saints and great men.

Ustad: Hey, I know everything, that's why I am an Ustad and you are a Jamura.

*Ustad and Jamura - street players

Shop Keeping

(In the evening, Ustad and Jamura are walking together in the market and talking.)

Jamura: Which shop is that saffron-colored glow signboard hanging on?

Ustad: Jamura, that is a temple of Sankatmochan.

Jamura: And Ustad, which shop is that with something written in blue letters that looks like a hotel menu. Is it an ice cream parlor?

Ustad: No, Rey. It is a Goddess temple, and the menu shows the rate of the earthen lamps in the temple.

Jamura: Ustad, I cannot understand why there is a need for glow signboards on temples?

Ustad: Jamura, this is also a form of shop keeping.

*Ustad and Jamura - street players

Caste feeling

Today we are celebrating Ambedkar Jayanti. All the intellectuals are gathered here for meaningful discussions. I am Anjali Sharma, a correspondent of an English newspaper. For the column "View", I need your views on Dalit empowerment.

"Mister, would you please give me your introduction?" 'I am Ramanand Shukla. (in a proud voice)'

"Oh! Wow! I am also a Brahmin...by the way, which kind of Brahmin are you?"

'We are Kanyakubja Brahmin.'

"From where?"

'Originally, we are from Uttar Pradesh but for the past four generations we have been living here.'

"Wow! That means you can make wedding relations with U.P. residents. I have an elder sister... please tell me any government employee groom for her."

'Aji, madam, due to these Dalits and OBCs, we Brahmins are not getting any government jobs.'

"Yes, you are absolutely right."

A Dalit thinker - Yaar... you are having discussions on your personal matters. This is not a suitable time for this kind of discussion.

Correspondent - Looking at the same caste, the caste feeling has come automatically. Well, I have collected enough material for my column. Kindly tell me your names only. I will prepare the article myself... Mr.. Ramanand Shukla, please give me your postal address and mobile number.

*Brahmin - Top upper caste ; Dalit -untouchable caste ; OBC - backward class;

Ambedkar - A great leader of Dalits who provided them reservations in government sectors;

Jayanti - Birth ceremony

Business

Jamura - Ustad, I have been playing the Damru (small drum) for the last two hours, but people are not gathering.

Ustad - Jamura, it seems we should wind up our business.

Jamura - Why, Ustad?

Ustad - Abey, so many other businessmen have come into this business and the competition is getting tough day by day. Someone is playing a drum named *"Jannat Se Jehad Tak."* Somewhere "Ghar-Vapsi" and conversion are both happening together. Someone is planning the deconstruction of the Masjid. Sometimes a bomb is placed in the temple. These people are too foolish to follow.

Jamura - Take it easy, Ustad. The taste of the people has changed. Nowadays, the business of astrology is booming. Let us start this business. We can bring a parrot and train it to pick up a paper... that's it.

Ustad - Abey, once I brought up a parrot for this purpose.

Jamura - Then what happened, Ustad?

Ustad - I had taught it to memorize some Shlokas from the Geeta and Ayats from the Quran.

Jamura - Then?

Ustad - People started worshiping him like a god, and one day he passed away. Communal riots broke out in the town. Hindus claimed that his last words were a Shloka, while Muslims argued that it was an Ayat.

Jamura: Then what happened, Ustad?

Ustad : An agreement was reached, and the Toteshwar Temple and Miyan Mitthu Ki Mazar were built.

Jamura : Ustad, when will peace be sustained in the world or will people continue to be killed in the name of religion in different communal riots?

Ustad: Jamura, peace can only be sustained when people change themselves or change their religions like clothes.

*Ustad and Jamura - street players ; Shloka- Sanskrit stanza

The End

About the Author

Alok Kumar Satpute

Alok Kumar Satpute has been writing fiction for many years. He has published nine books in Hindi with reputable publishing houses. His work, "Apne Apne Talibaan," has been translated into languages such as Urdu, English, and Marathi. His stories have been featured in newspapers and magazines across SAARC countries, including India, Pakistan, Nepal, and Bangladesh.)

His published books are-

Apne apne taliban, Baital fir daal par, Mohra Bachcha log taali bajaega, Moksh, Devdasi Premyoga,Chhoone se bikhar jaunga and Khat khula rahane diya (Hindi) Jihad (English and Marathi) Apne apne Taliban (Urdu)

www.ingramcontent.com/pod-product-compliance
Lightning Source LLC
LaVergne TN
LVHW041841070526
838199LV00045BA/1389